Also by Holly and Kelly Willoughby

Summer Holiday Mystery

School
for
Stars

Holly & Kelly
Willoughby

Orion
Children's Books

First published in Great Britain in 2014
by Orion Children's Books
a division of the Orion Publishing Group Ltd
Orion House
5 Upper St Martin's Lane
London WC2H 9EA
An Hachette UK Company

1 3 5 7 9 10 8 6 4 2

The Orion Publishing Group's policy is to use papers
that are natural, renewable and recyclable products and made
from wood grown in sustainable forests. The logging and
manufacturing processes are expected to conform to the
environmental regulations of the country of origin.

A catalogue record for this book is
available from the British Library

Printed in Great Britain by Clays Ltd, St Ives plc

ISBN 978 1 4440 0817 3

www.orionbooks.co.uk

For girls who crave adventure. What better place to start than in your mind? Just let your imagination run wild and who knows, maybe you'll write a book of your own adventures one day.

Contents

Dear Story-seeker,

So what's next we hear you ask? L'Etoile is closed for the summer holidays. What could our girls possibly be up to now?

Well you know, as we do, Story-seeker, that adventures don't only happen during term time. Just because our heroines, Molly, Maria, Sally and Pippa aren't sharing a room at Garland doesn't mean that they aren't getting up to mischief together elsewhere.

So join us at the Fitzfoster family country home by the sea, where Molly and Maria have returned from filming in America, ready for a rest. But with Sally and Pippa at their side and a seaside mystery to unravel, it's not likely to be much of a rest for any of them.

Are you ready, Story-seeker, to dive into the girls' summer holiday adventure? Because we're ready to share our story with you.

So sit tight and as they say at sea, 'Bon Voyage'.

Love,
Holly & Kelly Willoughby x

1

Homeward Bound

'Mooo-llly,' Maria whispered gently in her sister's ear. Molly didn't stir.

'Maria, please don't wake your sister just yet,' Mrs Fitzfoster said. 'The poor thing's been non-stop since we left for Hollywood four weeks ago. Let her sleep – at least until we get home, then she'll be fresh as a daisy for whatever seaside mischief awaits you two rabbits!'

Maria looked thoughtful for a moment and then smiled to herself at the thought of the adventures that lay ahead. And, boy, was she ready for some fun. As their mum said, life had been a complete whirlwind since she and the girls had moved to Los Angeles a month earlier, to accompany Molly while she filmed the latest Warner Brothers movie blockbuster.

They'd had such a fabulous time. Hollywood was every bit as glamorous as the girls had dreamed it would be. It was all so new and exciting for them both, and while Molly was busy learning scripts and shooting scenes, Maria had been at her side, ghostwriting a daily 'Mollywood' blog so that their friends back at home could keep up with everything that was happening. As you can imagine, this had left the girls and their mum completely exhausted and ready to relax at home.

And, even more importantly, they'd get to spend some time with their dad who'd only been able to join them in Hollywood for the first few days, due to his work commitments in London. This week however, he'd cancelled all his appointments and promised to be there, at Wilton House, so they could have some real family time together.

Although you know, Story-seeker, as Mr Fitzfoster did, that he wouldn't see his beloved girls for dust, if they had a sniff of an adventure!

'MOOOO-LLLY!' Maria squealed, and this time Molly nearly leapt out of her seat.

'What is it? Where's my script?' she exclaimed, mid-dream.

'Don't be daft, Moll, Maria smiled, feeling slightly guilty for having shouted quite so loudly. 'We're home Molly. No more scripts, no more early starts, just sunshine, the beach and plenty of midnight feasts with Sally for us.'

Molly looked as though she was about to burst into tears. She was tired and emotional, what with jet lag and the crazy schedule they'd all been living these past few weeks, but more than that, she'd missed home, her dad and her friends.

As the Fitzfoster Bentley bounced gently up the driveway, Wilton House came into view. The sprawling, yet welcoming, sandy coloured house took their breath away as it always did when they first pulled up for a visit.

'Hello, dear Wilton,' Mrs Fitzfoster murmured, matching her children's excitement.

Wilton House had the extraordinary luxury of

being the only house for miles, cushioned by fields and landscape views on one side, while the gardens at the rear ran down to the cliff edge which dropped away to the Sussex coast below. It truly was the most stunning place.

'Daddy!' Molly and Maria called out of the window.

Their chauffeur, the ever-obliging Eddie, stopped slightly short of his normal parking spot, nervous that the girls might actually jump out of the moving car in their excitement to be home. No sooner had he done so than Molly and Maria flew into their dad's arms, smothering him with hugs and chatter.

'Hello, my mischievous girls,' he said, grinning the same Fitzfoster smile he saw on his girls' faces.

'Hello,' he said, giving his wife a look which told her how much he'd missed her too. Linda Fitzfoster smiled happily back.

'Now girls, let's see, what surprises do I have in store for you?' Mr Fitzfoster said. 'Hmmmm, where to begin, I know, how about this for starters . . . '

And at that point, Sally came running out of the house with none other than their fourth partner in crime, Pippa Burrows. Molly and Maria shrieked with excitement. They were over the moon to see their friends. They'd known Sally would be there since their parents had hired her mum as their new housekeeper, but to see Pippa too, completed their world.

'Oh, Sally, Pippa. I've missed you both so much!' Molly flung her arms round them in a group hug.

'Pips, when did you get here?' Maria asked. 'How long are you staying?'

'Love your dress, Pippa,' Molly interrupted, suddenly spotting Pippa's gorgeous blue summer frock.

'Aaaah, too many questions at once!' Pippa said, giggling. 'But I think I can manage. I got here this morning. Sally fixed it with your mum over email to make this week the best ever before we go back to school. I'm here until Miss Hart's wedding to Mr Fuller next Sunday and then, if we're lucky and behave ourselves, your dad's said he might send Eddie to collect me from there so we can all go back to L'Etoile together on Monday.'

'Amazing! Thanks, Mum! Thanks, Dad! Thanks, Sal! You're the best!' Molly exploded with happiness.

'Hello, girls,' said another familiar voice. Sally's mum, Maggie Sudbury, appeared on the porch with a silver tray laden with scrummy-looking pink drinks.

'Maggie! How are you Maggie? Are you loving being at Wilton? Can't tell you how relieved we are to be back,' Molly said in a flurry, giving Maggie a gentle kiss on the cheek so as not to knock the drinks flying.

'Oh, my goodness, is that what I think it is?' Molly said, drooling at the thought. 'Is that *the* home-made pink lemonade Sally's been telling us about since we met?'

Maggie blushed almost the same pink as the glasses she was carrying. 'It is indeed, Molly. Welcome home, family Fitzfoster. Now would you like to follow me for more yummy snacks on the terrace?'

'Would we?' Maria cried. 'Wooohoo! We're home!'

And with that, the whole clan disappeared into Wilton House, ready for their summer holiday to really begin.

'As much as I don't wish to be a party pooper, I think that's quite enough pink fizz for one day, Molly darling,' said Mrs Fitzfoster having watched her daughter guzzle her third glass.

Before Molly could protest, Mr Fitzfoster, keen to tell his daughters about the next part of their surprise, said, 'Girls, if you've finished with this delicious spread, the lovely Maggie has prepared,' (Maggie blushed lemonade pink again, when he said that). 'Then I have another surprise for you.'

Immediately all four girls jumped up with glee. Maria was wracking her brains to try and think what her dad might have arranged for them. A sailing trip maybe? A trampoline?

'Maria, not even you will guess this one,' Mr F said, picturing the cogs whirring around in his clever daughter's head. 'Sally, dear, would you go and grab the key?'

'You aren't going to believe this!' Sally said, disappearing into the house and returning with a small silver key on an enormous gold star key ring.

'Thank you, Sally. Follow me, girls,' Mr Fitzfoster instructed, as he led them away from the house, down the garden path towards the sea.

'Mum, do you know what it is?' Molly asked.

'Why of course, darling. Dad and I have been plotting with Sally and Maggie the whole time we've been away. It's a little congratulations gift for everything you two girls have achieved since starting at L'Etoile last September.'

'Can you believe a whole year has passed already?' Pippa said, as she nearly took a tumble.

'Enjoy your trip?' Sally giggled and everyone burst out laughing.

As they emerged from the wooded area at the end

of the garden, the girls saw the most beautiful wooden house standing in its own perfect little manicured garden, complete with white fence and entrance and an outside dining area.

'Oh, my goodness, Mum, Dad, it's so beautiful!' Molly exclaimed. 'It's like a doll's house for grownups!'

Mr Fitzfoster chuckled. 'That was exactly the brief I gave Maggie and your mum. We wanted to give you girls your very own space so that you have somewhere 'parent free' to hang out.'

'Hang out?' Maria cried. 'Are you kidding? We're never leaving!'

The girls opened the gate to their new home and Molly spotted the plaque above the front door. *Hotel L'Etoile*. 'Ooooooh!' she gasped. 'So clever. Come on, L'Etoilettes, let's explore.'

As they hurried through the entrance, Mr Fitzfoster put his arm around his wife's shoulder, delighted by the girls' happy reaction.

'Have fun, my l'Etoilettes. See you in the morning.'

2

Living the Life of Luxury

Hotel L'Etoile was literally the most wonderful place ever. Set on two levels with a lounge/TV area, small kitchenette and bathroom downstairs and a spiral staircase to the upper floor with four beds and wardrobes. It was like a proper home.

'Can you believe this place?' Molly said to Pippa. 'How lucky are we?'

'Sally, you must have worked so hard to do all this. And you've thought of everything – from the massive comfy sofa, big enough for us all to squidge up on and chat or watch movies, to the high-tech study area for me to do my thing. You're so clever!' Maria added.

'Ah, I'm so relieved you like it. I can't take all the

credit though. Between me, Mum and Mrs F, the ideas never stopped coming. It's been such fun, honestly. The biggest problem was trying to find space for everything we thought you might need.'

'It's perfect,' Pippa said, looking around. Suddenly her Uncle Harry's recording studio looked very much like the shed it was, compared to this palace. 'I'm just so happy to be here!'

'Likewise! Four beds for four BFF's!' Molly said. 'Shall we go up to the house and get our stuff? We've got presents for you from LA – I'm dying to give them to you.'

'Yes, let's,' Maria answered, starting to put her sandals back on.

Knock Knock.

'I'll get it,' Pippa said.

As she opened the door, she saw a large man with a weather-beaten face, laden with suitcases.

'Hiya, girls. Thought we'd run your luggage down for you. Looks like you've been doing some serious shopping in America,' he said, as he heaved one of the bigger cases over the doorstep.

'Amazing! Hi, Malcolm. How are you? You must be a mind-reader. We were about to come and get everything,' Maria answered. 'Just chuck it in here and we'll sort out what needs to go up to the bedroom.'

'Anything for you, Miss Molly,' he grunted again.

Malcolm staggered in and put everything next to Maria's desk. His handsome son, Tom, followed with more luggage. 'Good to have you girls back,' Tom said. 'Gets a bit old around here without you!'

'Ah thanks, Tom! We're happy to be back! We plan on having lots of fun this week!' said Molly.

'Who was that?' Pippa asked.

'Malcolm and Tom. They look after Wilton House all year round as we're not always here. They do the same sort of things that Mr Hart does at L'Etoile... Anything from gardening to roof repairs.'

'Well they seemed lovely. In fact, is there anyone in the Fitzfoster world who isn't super nice? You really are the luckiest girls you know, and Sally and I are the luckiest BFFs in the world!' Pippa answered.

'Hear, hear!' Sally agreed. 'And isn't Tom gorgeous?'

'Right then! It's present time!' Molly said, her head buried in a pink spotty suitcase. 'This case is full of goodies from LA for you girls . . . Here's one for you Pips, one for you Sal . . . And Mimi, you've already seen yours, but here you go.'

The girls' eyes lit up as they each received their very

own vanity case, complete with a gold star on the top and their initials printed on.

'Oh, my goodness, Molly – it's beautiful!' Pippa said.

'Yes thanks, Fitzfosters – I love it!' Sally joined in.

'Look inside,' Molly instructed, and as they turned their keys, the lids sprang open to reveal a treasure trove of all the latest make-up, and a red t-shirt with a large gold star printed in the middle.

'Hope you like it. I only had one afternoon off from filming the whole time we were there so Mimi, Mum and I headed straight for the mall to get these fab t-shirts printed and stock up on make-up goodies for next term.'

'Apart from the star necklace you gave me, it's the best present I've ever had,' Sally said, trying on a pink *Lushylips* lipgloss. 'What do you think?' she said pouting in Maria's direction.

'Perfect' Maria said, delighted that the others would be engrossed in trying out every shade in their new collection, and wouldn't notice her devoting the next hour to setting up her techie corner of the room.

'Do you realise, we've not caught up on a single thing since we arrived. There's so much to talk about,' Pippa said suddenly, admiring her new t-shirt in the mirror.

'Well, you know all my gossip from the film,' Molly answered as she tonged Sally's hair into huge ringlets. 'Wasn't Maria's Mollywood blog just genius!'

'Hilarious!' Pippa and Sally said together, at which the giggles began all over again.

'I laughed out loud when I read about that director's wig blowing off when he turned the wind machine on by accident,' Pippa added.

'Oh, yes, I'd forgotten all about that,' Molly said.

'Ha! Talking of wigs, remember when we discovered old Ruby wears wigs too, that night when we were on our mission to find the *Lost Rose?*' Maria said.

'Oh, don't!' Sally said, clutching her sides. 'That was one of the funniest things I've ever heard.'

'Talking of blogs, Mimi, have you done your week's work experience with Luscious Tangerella yet? Wasn't that supposed to be this summer?' Pippa asked.

'Yes. But we couldn't fit it in with being in LA for so long, so I'm booked in to do it after we break up in December, in the week before Christmas. I reckon that'll be such a cool time too, think of the celeb Christmas party gossip there'll be,' Maria said. 'Besides, the Mollywood blog gave me some really valuable reporting experience as the production team said I could interview whoever I wanted, as long as they weren't on camera at the time.'

'That's something to look forward to at the end of the year then. And thanks, Maria, for being so unselfish and putting my needs before yours . . . Again!' Molly said giving her sister a hug.

Suddenly, Maria had a brainwave. 'What do you say we save the rest of our gossip for a midnight feast and nip for a quick swim in the pool now?'

'You have a pool?' Pippa said.

'And about ten gorgeous cozzies to choose from,' Molly said, smiling. 'Great idea, Mimi. Come on!'

'Tell me you've got about ten gorgeous swimming hats to choose from too, will you?' Sally said, concerned about her beautifully curled hair.

'Ha! Sure we do!' Molly laughed. 'They don't call us the *Fix-fosters* for nothing you know.'

'They do?' Maria asked, quite liking the nick-name.

'No, silly . . . But we could start the rumour,' Molly answered.

And with that, the four super-friends ran off up to the pool for a summer's evening dip.

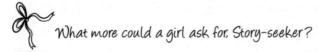 What more could a girl ask for, Story-seeker?

3

Over and Out

'That was the best night's sleep I've had all summer,' Molly said stretching.

'Ditto!' Pippa said, sitting up and looking at her watch.

'Are you joking?' Sally answered, her head still firmly under her feather pillow. 'Did none of you hear that weird growling and howling in the middle of the night?'

'No,' Molly and Pippa said.

'What do you mean howling and growling?' Molly asked, confused.

'Wasn't my stomach was it?' Pippa said rubbing her tummy. 'I ate far too many sweets last night – and as for your mum's chocolate brownies, Sally, I think I had the whole plate to myself!'

Sally smiled, loving that her mum's signature pink lemonade and chocolate brownies had been such a hit.

'No, honestly, it was like a weird animal noise. I've heard it before – when I first arrived at the start of the summer.'

'Well I never heard a thing. Sorry, Sal. Why don't you wake Maria up, she'll know what it was – in fact she probably already has a research pack on it,' Molly said.

Sally grabbed the bottom of Maria's duvet and gently pulled it back.

'She's not here!' Sally said.

'What do you mean, she's not here?' Molly said, slightly alarmed.

Right on cue they heard the key in the lock downstairs and in walked Maria, swinging four rucksacks behind her.

'Come on you lazy lot,' she called, seeing the three sleepy-heads peering down through the banisters at her. 'We've got a whole day of seaside fun ahead of us!'

'Wooohoo!' Molly yelled, throwing on her fluffy white dressing gown with her initials embroidered on the top pocket. Sally and Pippa were two seconds behind her in matching dressing gowns.

'What's in the rucksacks, Maria?' Pippa asked. Maria handed them out.

'While you lot have been snoring your heads off, I've been busy making us a picnic with Maggie. Boy, can that lady cook!' Maria said, giving Sally a thumbs up.

'But don't open those boxes yet as some of the bits are still warm, so better to keep them that way until we're ready to stuff our faces!'

'Owwww,' Pippa groaned at the thought of more food, only to be distracted by Molly rummaging through her rucksack and tossing a bottle of sun cream to one side.

'And what in glitter's name is this?' she said, pulling out a very high-tech and ugly-looking watch.

Maria laughed. 'OK, I know you won't believe me, as this is so something I'd come up with, but it turns out I am completely my father's daughter. He called me as I was leaving and dragged me up to his study for a lecture about safety and communication – the outcome of which is that we must each keep one of these on us at all times!'

'You have to be kidding me. As if I'm going to

wear something this . . . this . . . thing!' Molly said, despairing that it was so ugly. 'And besides, I've got a perfectly gorgeous watch, thank you.'

'Not like this one you haven't,' Maria answered, excited to show what the little gadget could do. 'It's a watch, but it's also a state-of-the-art walkie-talkie. You can be miles apart and it'll still work and let you talk to each other.'

'I was right, this is a joke. I'm with you all the time, Mimi, why do I need a flipping walkie-talkie, FGS?' Molly said

 FGS = for goodness sake, Story-seeker.

'It's no joke, Mol. You know what Dad's like about safety,' Maria said.

'I think it's cool!' Pippa answered, twiddling every knob she could find. 'I just haven't got the first clue how to use it.'

'That's easy. The biggest thing to remember is to make sure we're all on the same channel,' Maria continued.

'Come again?' Molly said, exasperated.

'Look like this . . . ' Maria showed the girls how to move through the ten available channels, stopping at channel seven. Then she showed them which button to push and hold down to talk, then release to listen for a response.

'Just remember though, girls, whenever you hold down that talk button on channel seven, Dad, Mum and Maggie can hear everything you're saying.'

'And half the Sussex police force knowing Dad!' Molly said, starting to see a funny side. 'He's so sweet isn't he? He always thinks we're going to get into a scrape.'

'Don't know what gave him that impression,' Pippa replied, rolling her eyes at the thought of getting into more Fitzfoster trouble!

Maria continued over the banter. 'Just so long as we check in with *whoever* is listening to let them know we're safe at least twice a day, I reckon we'll be able to explore where we like and come home when we like.'

'OK, I take it back . . . This is wicked!' Molly said, holding down the speech button and pressing her lips to the watch face.

'Moll-lly!' Maria said in alarm. 'They'll have just heard. . . '

'JOLLY GLAD TO HEAR YOU APPROVE, MISS MOLLY,' came a deep voice through all four of their watches at once. 'NOW BE SURE TO

BEHAVE YOURSELVES AND STAY IN RADIO CONTACT AT ALL TIMES! OVER.'

'ROGER THAT, DAD,' Maria said. 'WE PROMISE, OVER.'

'I KNOW I CAN COUNT ON YOU MARIA, OVER AND OUT BEAR CUBS.'

'Molly you really are a ditz, you know. We have to at least appear not to be treating this thing as a joke!'

'I know, I know. I'm sorry. But on one condition . . . Instead of using all that silly talk like *roger this* and *over and out that,* can't we use C4N or HAK?' Molly pleaded.

'Translation, please?' Pippa asked.

'Ciao for now . . . And Hugs and Kisses,' Molly said triumphantly, loving a little morning wind up sport with her sister.

Maria didn't even comment. Gosh, Molly could be annoying sometimes. Hilarious, but annoying!

4

Going for a Walkie-Talkie

Now Story-seeker, if anyone had been watching
as our four BFFs skipped along in their matching red
and gold star t-shirts, rucksacks, short white shorts
and sandals, they couldn't help but smile. It was
like an unofficial summer camp uniform with
Molly's style stamped all over it.

'Are we really walking all the way down there?'
Pippa asked, suddenly remembering she
didn't have a great head for heights.

'Yup!' Maria answered. 'You'll love it when you get
down there, Pips. I promise. It's like being on your own

shipwreck island – not another living soul for miles.'

'She's right, Pippa. Come on, link arms and we'll climb down together. This top bit's the worst actually. The stairs aren't so steep once you get to that viewing platform down there. From there they start to wind across the cliff rather than plummet straight down.'

'I can't believe we've got our own private beach for the day,' Sally said as the girls started their descent. 'How cool is that?'

'I know! It's only accessible from these cliff steps, or by boat from the next bay along, but the locals know it's private so no-one ever comes here,' Molly said.

'Plus the fact they'd be trespassing if they did. Dad would go ballistic if he thought anyone else was here. It would be easy for them to get to the house up these steps so it makes him a bit nervous.'

'He's not the only one who's nervous,' Pippa said, clinging to Molly. 'I hate heights.'

The girls felt as if they were on the edge of the world as they ventured down the uneven stone steps.

'Just a bit further, Pippa, and then we can have a rest on the viewing platform,' Molly coaxed gently.

'I can't believe you've been here all summer and not been down to our beach already, Sal,' Maria said, taking a deep breath of sea air.

'Well, part of me thought I'd save the excitement for when you got home. But to be honest, there hasn't been time. Hotel L'Etoile has taken every second of the holidays,' Sally answered, jumping down onto the decked, viewing platform.

'And a fine job you did too! In fact, you should have first go at looking through the telescope,' Molly said.

'Cool!' Sally said and ran over. 'This is brilliant – you can see for miles!'

'Do you want to have a look, Pips?' Sally offered.

Pippa, whose back hadn't left the rockface for a second, shook her head as she tried to fake a smile. She couldn't wait to get down to the bay!

'Mimi, quick, we need to do something to distract Pippa. She looks as if she's going to pass out!' Molly whispered to her sister.

'Right,' Maria nodded, wracking her brains.

'So Pips, you haven't told us anything about your summer? Have you done your auction prize with Alice yet?'

If you remember, Story-seeker, Pippa's auction promise was the chance to write and record a song with her Uncle Harry, and even to get Mr Fuller's input.

'Oh, girls, it was such a brilliant few days,' she said, stepping forward with a big grin.

Maria, you genius! Molly thought.

'Why, what happened?' Sally said quickly to keep Pippa talking and her mind off the dizzying drop.

'Well, Alice came down to the studio with her dad, big Al Parks. She was so relaxed – not at all nervy like she is at L'Etoile. She really let her hair down, and in the end we came up with a super track called *Fearless.*' Pippa pulled her rucksack off and started rummaging around for her iPod. 'Oh, bother, I could have sworn I packed it. Never mind, I'll play it to you later. You won't believe her vocal. Even Mr Fuller was impressed!'

'I'm so glad. If anyone deserves it, it's Alice. Can't wait to hear it.'

'Come on, we'd best get moving. My tummy's rumbling. The sooner we get down to the bay, the sooner we can break into this amazing picnic!' Maria said.

As the girls continued their journey down the cliff, they relaxed a bit. The stairs weren't so steep, which meant they could chat as they went, rather than using every ounce of energy concentrating on not tripping up.

Just as they were about to jump onto the sand, a voice echoed from their watches.

'COME IN BROWN BEAR CUB ... THIS IS PAPA BEAR CALLING ... ARE YOU RECEIVING BROWN BEAR CUB ... OVER.'

Maria pushed the talk button on her watch. 'ROGER THAT, PAPA BEAR. GO AHEAD ... OVER,' she said, as clearly as she could.

'JUST THOUGHT I'D CHECK IN WITH YOU BEAR CUBS AND SEE HOW THE EXPEDITION IS GOING. I HOPE YOU'RE TAKING CARE ON THOSE STEPS ... OVER,' Mr Fitzfoster said.

'ALL FINE, PAPA BEAR. YOUR CUBS HAVE IN FACT JUST REACHED THE BAY ... OVER,' Maria answered.

'HAS PINK BEAR CUB MADE IT WITHOUT HAVING TO RE-DO HER WINDSWEPT HAIR?' Mr Fitzfoster teased. Molly frowned.

'HA! WE'RE ALL IN PERFECT SPIRITS, PAPA BEAR. NO NEED FOR CONCERN ... OVER.'

Then a softer voice came over the speakers.

'GLAD TO HEAR IT, BEAR CUBS. BE SURE TO LEAVE THE BAY BY 4PM SO THAT YOU DON'T GET CAUGHT OUT

BY THE TIDE COMING IN . . . OVER,' said Mrs Fitzfoster.

'ROGER THAT, MAMA BEAR . . . OVER,' said Maria.

'HAK . . .' Molly joined in.

'HAK?' Mr Fitzfoster asked, bemused.

'HUGS AND KISSES . . . OVER.'

There was a sigh from both their parents and then silence.

'Molly, you crack me up,' Sally said. 'There's no changing Mollywood, is there?'

'Not likely, Sally,' Molly said smiling. 'Now that's quite enough exercise for one morning, let's crack this picnic open!'

Fed and pink lemonaded, the girls spread out to explore the bay. Maria had made them all switch to channel three so that they could have their own private communication line – without parental eavesdropping.

Sally headed straight for the rock-pools. She remembered her mum taking her crabbing many summers ago. They'd tied bits of bacon onto homemade fishing lines to entice the crabs out – but they always put them back, of course.

Pippa found the prettiest, quietest place she could and got out her notepad and voice recorder. If Wilton Bay couldn't inspire some seriously beautiful lyrics and melody, nowhere could.

Molly and Maria, predictably, as twins will be twins, Story-seeker, kicked off their designer strappy sandals and went for a paddle together, kicking and splashing around in the cool sea water. It truly was a glorious summer's day.

'Look, what's that, sticking out of the sand over there?' Molly asked.

'Where?' Maria said, looking across the bay.

'Here, look,' Molly answered, running over to it.

'It looks like an enormous egg!' Maria said, her voice tinged with excitement.

'Don't touch it,' she said, looking up. 'If its mother is circling somewhere, I don't fancy our chances. It must be a pretty big bird to have laid an egg that size.'

While Molly radioed Sally and Pippa to come and see what they'd found, the ever-inquisitive Maria took out her phone and snapped some pictures of the large, blueish white egg to help with her research that evening.

'The poor thing. What should we do? We can't just leave it here,' Molly said.

'I don't see what else we can do really. I don't fancy our chances of getting it back up to the house in one piece. Let's ask Dad about it later on. He'll know what to do for the best.'

Reluctantly, the girls headed back to their picnic and finished the last of the pink lemonade.

'What's next, a quick sunbathe and then start making our way back up to the house? I know mum said 4pm but we don't want to cut it too fine. Besides I fancy another swim in our nice warm pool. We'll get frostbite if we try and swim down here.'

'Perfect!' Molly agreed.

'Even better!' Molly cried and began covering herself in sun-cream. 'Now let's see if you can live up to your name brown bear cub . . . Over.'

'How did your songwriting go, Pips?' Sally asked as the girls were getting ready for supper back at Hotel L'Etoile.

'Brilliant. Talk about inspiration. I just might have a summer hit on my hands,' Pippa said excitedly.

'Talking about summer hits, Maria and I are dying

to hear the song you're singing for the wedding on Sunday. Can we pleeeeease?'

Pippa glowed with pride. 'I can't believe the wedding is next Sunday! I'm a mixture of *can't wait* and *scared stiff*. The only good thing is that I know Mr Fuller loves the song. I played it to him when we were in the studio with Alice and I'm sure I saw a tear in his eye.'

'Play it for us won't you . . . even better, sing it for us!' Molly pleaded.

'What now? I don't have any backing track for it as I'm doing it with a concert pianist. Then they're having a whole swing orchestra for the evening dancing. The music at this wedding is going to be out of this world!' Pippa said.

'Oh, go on, just sing us the chorus then,' Molly asked again.

'All right. Ready?' Pippa asked, and began to sing.

Just you and I
Our lives entwined
Begin our story together
Just you and I forever
Through love
True love

'Oh, Pippa, how romantic. What beautiful words. You're so clever,' Molly said.

'Now that's what I call out of this world,' Sally cooed. 'I just hope you won't run out of lyrics for when it's time for my wedding song.'

'Ha! I'll never run out of words,' Pippa said, giggling. 'But we all just might run out of lives if we continue getting into as much mischief as we seem to.'

'Mischief? Us? Don't know what you mean,' Maria answered, looking up from her laptop where she'd been scanning the internet since they'd got back from the beach for information about the egg they'd found.

She was sure there was an adventure here somewhere, Story-seeker, and she, Maria Fitzfoster, was hot on its tail.

♡ ♥ ♡

5

Reunited with Friends

'Who are the extra two places for, Mum?' Molly asked as the girls took their seats around the table on the terrace.

'You'll see,' Mrs Fitzfoster answered, winking at Mr Fitzfoster who was standing at the head of the table, opening a bottle of champagne.

Molly, Maria and Pippa all looked over at Sally.

'What?' she said innocently. 'Don't look at me. I might have known everything about everything before you arrived, but I've been in your Molly and Maria bubble since then. I've no idea what's happening. Mum?' Sally called over to her mum.

But Maggie, who had been filling everyone's water glasses, was suddenly nowhere to be seen.

'Oooh, I love a surprise,' Molly said.

'Just so long as it's a good one,' Maria said in true *suspicious* Maria style. 'I know – let's play the best and worst game!'

'What's that?' Sally asked.

'You know, where you imagine the best and worst possible outcomes to a situation.' Molly said, thinking.

'Well that's a no brainer! The worst guests ever would be Lucifette and Lavinia! Just imagine if they walked in here now. I think I'd faint!' Pippa said.

Lucinda Marciano and her partner in crime Lavinia Wright were the meanest girls at L'Etoile, Story-seeker. Both girls had tried to ruin the girls' first school year on numerous occasions so to have them at this dinner party would be a living nightmare.

'Ah CO, Pips,' Molly exclaimed.

CO = chill-out, Story-seeker.

'There's more chance of you climbing down Wilton cliff blindfolded than those two horror-hogs turning up here for dinner.'

The girls all giggled, picturing a terrified Pippa, clinging to the rockface in the dark.

'I actually might prefer a blindfold!' Pippa said. 'Anyway you've got to admit, I was so much better on the way up wasn't I? I thought I made great progress.'

'You were brilliant, Pips. I'm only teasing. So we've had your worst, who would be your best guest then…' Maria continued.

'Shhhhh . . . they're here . . . whoever they might be!' Molly said hearing footsteps coming their way.

'MISS HART!' the four girls cried at once. 'MR FULLER!' they said, scrambling to their feet.

'It's so lovely to see you. But how have you found the time, Miss Hart – with only a week to go until the wedding?' Molly said, leading her favourite teacher to her seat.

'Mr Fuller and I thought it would be a welcome change to wedding chaos,' Miss Hart answered.

What a beautiful bride and CAC, Molly thought.

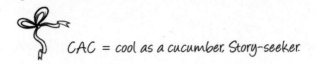

CAC = cool as a cucumber. Story-seeker.

'But how did this . . . Why did you . . . ?' Maria said, half-asking her father. As much as she was pleased to see Miss Hart and Mr Fuller, she couldn't figure out what would have prompted her parents to invite them.

'Oh, Maria,' Mr Fitzfoster began. 'You're always one step ahead aren't you? Well for your information, and not that we should need a reason to dine with such wonderful guests, but in this case, there is one more surprise for you . . .'

Suddenly, Maggie appeared on the terrace carrying a wriggling ball of excited, black fluff in her arms.

'TWINKLE!' the girls squealed.

'Oh, Twinkle, Twinkle, I've missed you soooooo much,' Maria said, burying her head in the puppy's fur.

It always surprised everyone seeing Maria melt into a puddle of emotion where animals are concerned. But animals, if you remember, Story-seeker, are Maria's one weakness in life.

'Twinkle! Haven't you grown . . . I thought you'd stopped but you haven't have you?' Molly said, taking her turn for a cuddle.

While Pippa and Sally fussed over Twinkle, Maria thanked Miss Hart.

'Oh, Miss Hart. Thanks so much for bringing her to see us. It's made my summer! Please stay the night so we can invite Twinkle to Hotel L'Etoile for a sleepover.'

Miss Hart laughed. 'While I can't even begin to imagine what Hotel L'Etoile is, I might be able to do a little better than that. Mr Hart has gone on a fishing trip to Iceland this week and what with Mr Fuller and I being busy with last minute wedding preparations, he and I wondered if you girls would do us an enormous favour and dog-sit until the start of term.'

The girls' eyes were wild with excitement.

'Dad?' Maria asked her father.

'It's fine, Mimi. We've already made all the necessary arrangements, and I think if you look under the sofa at Hotel L'Etoile, you'll find a dog bed all ready for Twinkle's stay.'

'Mum, Dad, you're the best!' Molly and Maria exclaimed.

'Twinkle, did you hear that? You're going to

stay with us for a whole week!' Molly whispered in Twinkle's ear.

'Woof, woof!' Twinkle barked her approval, making everyone laugh.

'Now, would you all be so kind as to take your seats please, so that we can toast the happy couple. To Mr and Mrs Fuller to be,' Mr Fitzfoster announced, raising his glass. There was a loud chinking of champagne and pink lemonade glasses.

What a supper of super-suprises!

Try saying that four times, quickly, Story-seeker!

♡

'We'll see Miss Hart and Mr Fuller to their car,' Molly said to her dad at the end of the evening.

'If you're sure, girls,' he said and turned to the happy couple. 'Linda and I look forward to seeing you on Sunday then, Emmett.'

'Absolutely!' Mr Fuller, said, shaking him warmly by the hand. 'And thank you for your wonderful hospitality this evening. I can only hope our wedding feast is just as delicious.'

Molly couldn't believe what she was hearing! How

could her mum and dad have forgotten to mention that they had been invited to the wedding of the century? She was absolutely green with envy. Not only would it have been her first ever wedding, but she would have loved to hear Pippa sing in the church.

'Bye, Miss Hart. Bye, Mr Fuller,' Maria said, holding open the car door. 'It's been such a lovely night.'

'And don't worry about Twinkle. She's in the best of hands!' Molly said.

'Good luck on Sunday, Miss,' said Sally, giving Miss Hart a hug. 'We'll be thinking of you.'

'Thank you for everything, girls. It's so lovely seeing you here together, looking after each other. That's how friendships should be,' Miss Hart said. 'And Pippa, dear, see you in the church. I can't wait to hear you sing. It will be a highlight for us both.'

'Me too,' Pippa agreed.

'Incidentally, Pippa,' Miss Hart added. 'If the girls aren't busy with some adventure or other on Sunday, why don't you bring them along? They'd be more than welcome.'

'Are you kidding?' Molly said, thinking she might burst with excitement.

'We'd love to!' Maria, Molly and Sally said at once.

'That's settled then. Goodnight, girls,' Miss Hart

6

An Egg-straordinary Find

'No Twinkle, please don't – anything but those – I haven't even worn them yet!' Molly cried, chasing the mischievous puppy around the bedroom.

'She's bored, Moll,' Pippa said, grabbing Molly's new sunglasses from Twinkle's mouth as she flew past.

'As am I, of you lot trying on clothes. If I have to give my opinion on one more outfit, I think I'll go crazy,' Maria said.

'What shall we do then?' Pippa asked, hoping the answer wouldn't involve any heights.

'Maria's right, Molly. All we've done is plan outfits and hairdos since we heard we were going to the wedding. Let's call it a day. I reckon these ones are spot on.'

'You think?' Molly asked, examining herself for the hundredth time in the mirror. Then she smiled. 'I'm not sure. I'll just call in a couple of extra things from www.looklikeastar.com in time for Albie's delivery tomorrow. Just in case we change our minds. And then we'll get some fresh air. We could even take Twinkle up to the pool for a swim. She'll love that.'

'She might, but Dad will go bonkers!' Maria said, still tapping away on her computer.

'What are you doing anyway, Maria? You've been squirrelling away on that laptop forever. Are you writing another blog or something?' Pippa asked.

'It's not a blog yet, but I've a feeling I'm onto something,' she answered. 'While you lot have been playing *changing rooms*, I've been looking up that egg we found on the beach but it's still a mystery – which is the exciting bit I guess. I've examined pictures of eggs from every species of bird you'd expect to find on the coast, but I've drawn a blank for an egg that size and colour.'

'So – what's exciting about finding nothing?' Molly asked.

'Think about it, if the egg was supposed to be there,

I'd have pulled up info on it straight away but there's nothing. How does an egg, the size of a dinosaur egg, come to be on our beach? It just doesn't feel right.' Maria said.

'I see . . . I guess you could say it's rather *un-egg-spected*,' Sally said with a smile at which point all the girls got the complete giggles.

'*Egg-citing* though!' Pippa said, feeling very pleased with herself.

'Yes, have a good laugh!' Maria said, trying her hardest to be serious. 'This thing's been eating me up. You know how I hate not finding the answer to something.'

'Sorry, Mimi,' Molly said, smothering a giggle. 'There's only one thing for it, you need to contact an *egg-spert*.'

'Very funny, sis,' Maria said above the hysteria. 'Don't you think I haven't already considered that? There's bound to be some bird-watching club in the village, but if we have found something *egg-straordinary*, I don't want them poking their beaks in! See we can all be witty!'

'Oh, stop it, my tummy aches from laughing,' Pippa said, clutching her sides.

'Besides, these photos I took on my phone aren't

great. It would have been so much better if we'd just brought the egg back with us – but couldn't risk the mother rejecting it.' Maria continued.

'You're right – and besides - I don't even want to imagine how big the mother bird is that laid an egg that size!' Molly said dramatically.

'If only we knew a keen bird-watcher, someone we could really trust' Pippa said trying to think. They had had such a laugh, but all the girls were aware that Maria was starting to get frustrated, and there was nothing worse than a frustrated Maria!

'Wait, that's it! Pippa you're a genius,' Maria exclaimed.

'I am?' Pippa said in surprise.

'Yes!' Maria said, giving her a hug. 'All this time I've been wracking my brains and trawling the internet to find answers, I forgot about human beings with knowledge!'

'Who?' Sally asked.

'Well actually, there are two people that spring to mind. Firstly, I'm pretty sure Malcolm's son Tom is a pretty keen bird watcher. And secondly there's dear old Mr Hart. I can't believe I didn't think of him right away.'

'Oh, yes! Tom's a brilliant shout. But not sure about

Mr Hart – it's a fishing trip he's gone on, not a bird-watching holiday!' Molly said.

'Yes, but the bookshelves in his study at L'Etoile are rammed with nature books, particularly bird books. I tell you what, if I'm wrong, I'll let you spend the rest of the day trying wedding outfits on me, Molly. Deal?' Maria asked, loving setting herself a challenge.

'You're on!' Molly smiled. 'Let's go and see Tom now. Hopefully he'll be able to help. You're forgetting Mr Hart's away. How are we going to get in touch with him on a boat in the middle of a lake in Iceland?'

'By email, silly! Yes, even Mr Hart's joined the technological revolution and has a smart phone! He was on all those *Legend of the Lost Rose* tours emails at the end of last term, when we were discussing the summer tours. I'm sure I've got it here somewhere . . .' She paused, tapping away through her email history. 'Yes, here we go . . . davidanthonyhart@l'etoile.co.uk. I'll try him first.'

Suddenly a voice came through the walkie-talkie watches which were lined up on charge on the desk.

'BEAR CUBS, THIS IS THE KITCHEN, ARE YOU RECEIVING? OVER.' It was Maggie's voice.

'HI, MUM . . .' Sally said and then. 'I MEAN, ROGER THAT CHEF . . . BEAR CUBS RECEIVING . . . GO AHEAD.'

'PIZZAS ON THE TERRACE IN TEN MINUTES, BEAR CUBS . . . AND IF YOU'RE QUICK YOU CAN SCATTER YOUR OWN TOPPINGS . . . OVER!' Maggie finished.

'DIVINE . . . BE WITH YOU IN TEN SECONDS, CHEF . . . OVER,' Molly said, grabbing her walkie-talkie.

Home-made pizza, Story-seeker?
Is there anything better?

'Did you hear that, Mimi? Scrumdiddlyumptious! You ready?' Molly called over to Maria who was putting the finishing touches to her email to Mr Hart.

'Just about. I'm putting a photo of Twinkle wearing your sunglasses in with the egg shots,' Maria said.

'What, when did she . . . Let me see . . .' Molly said in a panic.

'Just kidding!' Maria replied. 'But your face was a picture! Wish I'd got a photo of that!'

'Oh, come on – I've got ham, cheese, mushrooms, pepperoni and spaghetti on the brain!' Molly groaned.

'Spaghetti! On a pizza?' Sally asked, looking disgusted.

'Don't ask! She ate it by accident while she was filming in LA and has never stopped going on about it since. I mean pasta on a pizza, whoever heard of anything so ridiculous?' Maria said.

'What I put on my pizza is NOYB, Mimi, dearest!' Molly shouted as she raced out of the door.

'NOYB?' Pippa raised an eyebrow in Maria's direction, but before she could answer, Sally jumped in.

'None of your business! Am I right? Am I right?' she asked.

'Spot on, Sal! Finally someone else who speaks Mollywood!'

And the girls ran off to the terrace for lashings of spaghetti pizza.

'Can somebody carry me back?' Molly begged.

'Has someone eaten too many carbs?' Maria said, looking at her sister dragging her feet along the path.

'I have to admit, it did taste great though,' Pippa said.

But Maria's mind was on one thing and one thing

only – the egg! Had Mr Hart replied to her email? If not she'd have to find Tom.

'Where are you going, Mimi?' Molly said, as the garden path split in two directions.

'I'm going to run up and see if Tom's about to show him this egg photo on my phone. Usually you can hear him on the lawnmower somewhere, but it's all quiet today,' Maria said.

'I'll come with you,' Sally said.

'OK, Pips and I will go back to Hotel L'Etoile and have a tidy-up then,' Molly said, knowing full well all she wanted to do was collapse on the sofa in front of a good movie.

'Cool – text me if Mr Hart's replied, will you – I don't seem to be getting any emails through on my phone since arriving at Wilton,' Maria said. 'Let's go, Sal!'

'Hi, Malcolm,' Maria said, as she knocked and opened the caretaker's office door. 'Sorry to bother you – just wondered if Tom was about for a quick word.'

'No worries, Maria. But no, sorry, Tom's taken a couple of days holiday to spend time with friends. He won't be back at Wilton until Monday now,' Malcolm said, wiping his mouth. 'Anything I can do to help?'

Sally opened her mouth to tell Malcolm all about the egg, but Maria quickly interrupted her. 'No, no, we just wanted to show him something he was asking us about. It's not urgent. We'll see him before we go back to school no doubt. See you Malcolm . . . and thanks!' Maria said, dragging Sally out into the garden before she could say another word.

'What was all that about? Why didn't you just ask Malcolm? He might have known you know,' Sally asked.

'I know, but I could feel my mobile buzzing in my pocket meaning a text . . . And look, I was right! It's from Moll – Mr Hart's emailed back. Let's see what he's got to say first. I just feel like the fewer people who know about this for the moment, the better. Come on!' Maria said.

Molly handed Maria her laptop as soon as she walked through the door. She knew better than to open anything up.

'We haven't read it, Mimi. What does it say?'

There was a ping as she opened her laptop. *Inbox: 1 Unread Email*.

And she read out loud:

To: mariafitzfoster@l'etoile.co.uk
From: davidanthonyhart@l'etoile.co.uk

Dear Maria,

My heart leapt to see that brilliant picture of naughty Twinkle. Hope she's behaving herself while I'm away. I'm having a super time but miss her already. It makes things easier to know she's being looked after by the best dog-sitters on the planet!

Now onto a very serious note – the egg. I do hope you girls aren't up to any of your high jinks – especially when you hear what I've got to say. Unless I'm mistaken, it looks to me like an egg from a Californian Condor, which is a highly endangered species native to the Andes Mountains, so I can't even begin to imagine how it's come to be on your beach in Sussex!

Maria, I suggest you report your findings to the police immediately. Give them my contact details and explain I'm away but can assist and will be in touch next week after the wedding to get to the bottom of this.
Take care girls, and please, be very careful. The importation of endangered birds' eggs to England is

highly illegal, and not something you want to meddle in if it's happening in your area. An illegal collector would pay an absolute fortune to own an egg such as this. Keep your distance and let the police deal with it. Please write back and give me your word, Maria, or I shall worry.

Warmest regards,
David Hart

'I knew it!' Maria said, wide-eyed, already googling *Californian Condor*.

'I've never met anyone with a nose for trouble like you,' Pippa said, genuinely impressed.

'What does Google say, Mimi?' Molly asked, peering over Maria's shoulder.

'Oh, my, it's no wonder they're endangered,' she said. 'Says here that each Condor chooses one partner for its entire life. The female Condor lays just one egg and both parents then look after it until it can take care of itself.'

'What we going to do now then? You need to answer Mr Hart and let him know we'll do as he asks – even if you're thinking of keeping it to ourselves for now,' Molly said, knowing full well that her sister had no intention of sharing their secret just yet!

'Do you think we should contact the police? Mr Hart was pretty insistent about that, and he seems to know what he's talking about,' Sally said, thoughtfully.

Pippa and Molly nodded gently in agreement.

Maria was horrified. Finally, a bit of excitement in their own back garden and the girls wanted out! No way, not yet.

'Oh, come on, girls. Where's your l'Etoilette spirit? Don't you see? This is the summer adventure we've been waiting for. Our last chance for a bit of fun before school starts in a few days. What do you say – are you with me?'

Sally, Molly and Pippa turned to each other to whisper their concerns. Well, Molly and Pippa rather than Sally. This mystery felt a bit different to the *Lost Rose*. Then they were chasing a legend. This time, they might come up against some real life danger in the form of a smuggler. Someone brazen enough to be using Wilton Bay to smuggle illegal bird's eggs.

'But we've got to do something,' Sally pleaded, ready for a Fitzfoster adventure. 'We owe it to all those baby birds who might suffer the same fate.'

Maria was impressed with Sally's powers of

persuasion, and as frowns turned to smiles she knew the other girls were on board.

'Come on then, let's get cracking! Ha!'

'I just hope we don't end up with egg on our faces!' Sally said with a smile.

'No chance. And anyway, I don't *egg-spect* we'll find it again. The tide would surely have washed it away, then we'll have no evidence for the police apart from a couple of grainy, badly *egg-secuted* photos!'

'All right . . . all right . . . enough with the egg jokes. It's *egg-scrutiating*!' Molly joined in.

The girls threw on sweatshirts, feeling like the temperature had already dropped a bit since lunchtime, and grabbed their rucksacks and watches, ready for the long climb down the cliff.

'At least Twinkle's with us this time . . . She'll be able to sniff out any danger,' Sally said, cheerfully.

'That's *egg-sactly* what I'm banking on!' Maria cried, marching off with her fellow detectives in tow.

7

Calling All Agents

*P*ippa had pretty much held her breath until they reached the viewing platform. Why did she have to be the only one with vertigo? It was so frustrating.

Suddenly Maria said in her loudest whisper . . . 'STOP! Quick, stand against the cliff.'

Molly, Pippa and Sally threw themselves against the rock as though a bomb had gone off.

'What is it?' Molly said quietly.

'This had better be good. I think I've just aged forty years!' Pippa groaned.

'There's a boat in the bay,' Maria said, frowning.

'WHAT?' Molly said. 'But that's impossible! No-one's allowed to visit Wilton Bay without permission.

'I'm telling you, there's a blue and white motor boat, tied up in the bay,' Maria answered, craning her neck to try and see.

'Is there anyone on the boat?' Sally said, nervously.

'It all happened too quickly. I only saw the boat and immediately ducked, just in case there was someone on it. I didn't want them to see us before we saw them . . . not until we find out exactly who they are and what they're doing on our beach!'

'I say we go back to the house and come up with a plan there. We're like sitting ducks out here,' Sally suggested.

Maria liked her thinking and silently led her troops back to Hotel L'Etoile.

The girls were in a complete spin.

'Right, focus, Maria,' she said to herself out loud. 'Let's be methodical about this. First, we need to find out whether that boat had permission to be there. Sally, do you know how that usually works.'

'Not really. I can't remember anyone asking Mum about it since I've been home for the holidays – but thinking about it, there's a visitor's book by the kitchen door of any house comings and goings. Surely it would say there if it was a legitimate visit,' Sally answered.

'Brilliant, Sal. That's exactly where we need to start,' Maria said, ticking *action point one* off her list.

'I'll go up to the house now, get us a snack and sneak a peek at the book,' Sally said, disappearing out of the door.

'Next thing to work out is what if that boat has no permission, or reason to be in the bay? Is there anywhere up here where we can spy on the bay without having to go down to the viewing platform? I reckon we need to get out there straight away with some binoculars. It's crucial we try to get a look at whoever is on that boat!' Pippa said, the familiar feeling of Fitzfoster mischief adrenalin pumping around her body.

'Welcome back, Agent Burrows! Good to see you thinking like a true detective,' Molly grinned and turned to her sister.

'She's right, Mimi. What about up by Dad's favourite stone bench? There's a perfect view down to the bay from there. If we take some blankets and stay low to the ground, whoever's down there will never spot us.'

'Spot on. But hang on, without the telescope or any binoculars, we've got no chance of making out any faces, and I'm pretty sure the zoom on our camera won't pick up anything useful from that far away . . .' Maria had her thinking face on – which suddenly, lit up.

'I've got it! Back in a sec . . .' she said.

'And then there were two . . .' Pippa noted.

'Woof!' Twinkle barked.

'Sorry, Twinks – three, I meant three!' Pippa grinned.

Moments later Sally and Maria came back, chattering about their findings.

'Hem, hem,' Molly said. 'Would you mind bringing us up to speed with what's going on?' 'Sorry, sis!' Maria said. She was so excited by her latest gadget, she'd quite forgotten to include the others.

'Check this out!' she said, un-zipping a large black briefcase on the coffee table.

'Woooah! Where did you get that?' Molly asked in astonishment, quite certain that her parents hadn't suddenly become paparazzi photographers in the last year.

'Isn't it perfect? Come on, I'll tell you on the way. We can't risk missing that boat leave.'

The girls threw on some sweatshirts, grabbed a bundle of blankets and ran up to camp out by their dad's favourite stone bench.

'Please tell me it's still there,' Pippa called to Maria who'd reached the bench first.

'Yes!' she said, her eyes gleaming. 'Hurry up you lot, and take up your positions. We could be in for a long wait . . .'

'I've sorted that,' Sally said. 'Your mum was in the kitchen chatting to mine. I said we were having a girl's beauty night, complete with detox and face packs. Said they'd definitely want to avoid us until morning – unless they wanted to be greeted by mud-caked monsters!'

'Ha! Genius, Sally,' Molly said.

'Yeah – way to go, Sal,' said Pippa, picturing them all dripping in face mud.

'Um, should I be worried that we all seem to be getting far too good at bending the truth, special agents?' Maria asked.

'How cheeky!' Molly cried. 'You're the one who's

magicked up the state of the art, paparazzi camera with the longest lens in the world! How about an explanation of where you pulled that from Agent F1?'

Maria smiled. 'Remember that Summer Ball, Mum and Dad hosted last year? I happened to be there when security hauled a photographer out of the tree. He'd been spying on the guests trying to get photos to leak to the newspapers. The security guards confiscated his camera - this camera - while they were waiting for the police to arrive, but the photographer managed to escape, leaving it behind. It's been sitting in Dad's study ever since – just in case he ever tried to come back for it. His loss is our gain, I say!' she said, squinting through the lens and zooming in on the boat.

'Why Agent F1, your genius never fails!' Molly said.

'Can you see anything?' Pippa asked.

'Just the boat. My guess is that our mystery sailor will wait until dark. That's what I'd do, if I didn't want to risk being seen. It's bad enough having to leave the boat there in plain view.'

'Let's have a look, Mimi,' said Molly, grabbing the camera.

'Sure!' Maria said. 'Get comfortable agents. I think we're in for a long night!'

'Are you girls all right? It's getting cold out here.' Molly pulled her blanket around her.

'Not cold, so much as tired,' Sally groaned, struggling to keep her eyes open.

'It can't be too much longer,' Pippa said. 'It's been dark for over an hour now. Here, have some pink lemonade, the sugar will keep you awake.'

As Pippa pulled a flask from her rucksack, Maria suddenly wriggled as she looked through the lens. 'Shhhhhhh,' she whispered. 'There's someone on the beach . . . Actually make that two someones! There are two lights – two people!'

'Can you make out their faces, Mimi?' Molly asked quickly.

'Nooo!' said Maria. 'The one thing this stupid camera hasn't got is night vision.' She snapped a few shots of the bay anyway, hoping she might be able to lighten the images on her laptop later. 'Here, Pips, have a look,' she said, passing Pippa the camera.

'One of the lights - must be a torch - is staying on the beach, and the other is heading for the boat,' Pippa reported back.

'Oh, my goodness . . . What do we do if they don't both get on the boat? That means someone's been staying on our beach,' Maria said.

'And to think we were down there. I wonder if the one on the beach was watching us,' Molly said in a worried voice. 'But where would they have been hiding? You saw the bay, it's completely open!'

'It's no good. I need to get closer,' Maria said.

'Are you crazy?' Pippa said, handing back the camera.

'Yes, remember what Mr Hart said about them being dangerous people. It's too dangerous, Mimi,' Molly pleaded.

'I won't go all the way down – just to the viewing platform. If I don't at least try to get some decent photos we'll have completely wasted our time. I'll be careful,' Maria promised.

'Stuff it, I'm coming with you, sis!' Molly said.

'You sure, Moll? Two heads would be better than one, I have to admit, but no-one else or we'll risk being seen.' Maria turned to Pippa and Sally. 'Agents, switch walkie-talkies to channel three so we can get you in an emergency. You girls go back and check on Twinkle and we'll see you in a bit.'

'Be careful!' Sally and Pippa said together.

♡

'Stay close, Molly,' Maria whispered. They had to move quickly, but luckily both girls knew the cliff steps like the back of their hand.

'This is much better!' Maria whispered triumphantly, snapping some dark and grainy pictures from the shadows of the viewing platform. 'Only problem is I can't use the flash from here or they'll definitely spot us.'

'Oh, give it here, Mimi,' Molly hissed back, grabbing the camera. 'I just can't believe there's no night vision switch on this thing!'

'Hurry, Moll, or we'll lose them!' Maria said, watching the two torchlights bobbing around in the darkness below.

'Let's see now . . .' Molly paused, using the light from her dimmed torch to read the letters next to the buttons.

'IFRNV!' she cried, nearly forgetting to whisper! 'Just call me the queen of abbreviations! IFRNV – infra-red night vision.' She flicked the switch and zoomed in on the boat.

'It's working!' she whispered, snapping away.

'The one getting on the boat is a large man – but he's got one of those huge parker coats on with the hood pulled right up so you can't see his face . . . Bother and blast!' she reported back. Then she pointed the lens to the light moving on the beach. 'Oh, for goodness sake, the one on the beach is covered from head to toe too! WATC!'

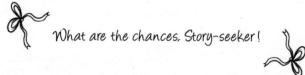

What are the chances, Story-seeker!

'He's much skinnier though.'

Maria grabbed the camera and looked through the lens. 'You're the brainbox tonight, Moll. Well done!'

'The boat's moving away with one on board, but the one on the beach is moving towards the rocks . . . He's carrying something – looks like a box of some sort.' Maria was silent for a moment, swinging the camera from left to right. 'Molly, he's gone.'

'What do you mean, he's gone? He can't have just disappeared, that's impossible. We know that bay – there's nowhere for him to go,' Molly said.

'Unless he's Mr Invisible, or he's grown a pair of wings and flown off the beach, he just did!' Maria answered, flabbergasted.

'Oh, no, you don't think he's coming up the cliff

steps do you?' Molly gasped, realising that they might be right in his path. 'I don't think we should take that chance, do you?'

'Nope. Come on, let's get out of here and see if we've got any decent photos. We'll work out what to do next with the others.'

And with that, the Fitzfoster twins scooted back up the rockface and home to tell Sally, Pippa and Twinkle all about it.

'Oh, thank goodness you're both all right,' Pippa said, trying to beat Twinkle to the girls as they arrived back. 'We didn't dare try to contact you via channel three in case our voices came over too loudly and gave your hiding place away.'

'Come over here and drink these, you're both half-frozen!' Sally said, passing them mugs of steaming hot chocolate complete with melting marshmallows.

'Thanks – quick, pass me my laptop,' Maria said, popping open the memory card compartment on the camera. 'Let's see what we've got.'

As the photos uploaded the girls saw about a hundred shots, some completely dark and then a few clearer, night vision-aided shots showing a large man getting into the boat and a skinny man on the beach carrying a box. As they feared, both of the men's faces were completely hidden by their enormous hoods.

'Grrrrrr . . . this is so frustrating. Even with the night vision, we're still none the wiser. And the worst of it is, the skinny man on the beach just vanished into thin air.'

'There's only one thing for it,' Sally announced. 'We are just going to have to go down to the beach tomorrow and check it out for ourselves.'

'I agree,' Molly said, sleepily. 'And we'll take Twinkle. If anyone can find that man with the box, she will. Won't you Twinkle-toes ?'

'Woof!' Twinkle barked, wagging her tail in excitement at the prospect of her own adventure.

'We'd best put in an appearance at breakfast, though, or Dad's going to wonder where we've been. Or, more importantly, what we've been up to. With everything that's been going on we've totally forgotten to radio him today. It won't have gone unnoticed!' Maria said with a groan.

'Don't worry about that, girls. Pips and I have already checked in to say that we've had such a relaxing pamper night and that you two couldn't talk in case you cracked your face packs!' Sally said.

8

The Plot Thickens

'*D*id Twinkle have tummy-ache in the night, darling?' Mrs Fitzfoster asked Molly at breakfast.

All four girls looked up, guiltily.

'I don't think so, Mum,' Molly answered. 'What makes you ask?'

'Only that I thought I heard her howling in the night. It was such a deep, growly howl I thought perhaps you'd given her too many treats,' Mrs Fitzfoster said.

'Not unless we slept through it,' Maria said, shooting the girls a look of alarm, and wondering what else they'd slept through – like a skinny man walking past their front door with a mystery box, for example!

None of the girls had heard a thing, but they'd been so exhausted after their night's detective work it was possible they'd all slept through it. Sally, however, was immediately reminded of the howling she'd heard the first night they'd stayed in Hotel L'Etoile. Twinkle hadn't even been at Wilton House then. It must be connected to the mystery on the beach. She couldn't wait to discuss it with the others.

Maria, noticing that Sally was looking twitchy, signalled to Molly and Pippa to eat up so they could get going. Just as the girls started to say their thank yous for breakfast, Mr Fitzfoster looked up from his newspaper.

'And what's on the agenda for today, my darlings? I should think you're starting to run out of ideas of what to do now aren't you?' he said, rather hoping.

'Not at all, Dad,' Maria said, moving towards her father. 'In actual fact, we've only been down to the beach once since we arrived. We thought that seeing as the sun is shining and the wind has dropped, we'd pop down again today with one of Maggie's wonder-picnics.'

The girls nodded in agreement and Maggie disappeared to the kitchen to cobble together some lunch for them.

Nothing like a bit of notice, girls! she thought.

'I see. Well, that all sounds wonderful, but you might have to re-think your plan. As of early this morning, the cliff steps are unfortunately out of bounds until further notice.'

'What?' they said in disbelief.

'Oh, dear me,' Mr Fitzfoster said, confused by the looks of devastation across the four faces in front of him. 'I hadn't realised you'd be quite this upset. Can't be helped though, I'm afraid. Perhaps you can picnic out in one of the fields? I could get Malcolm to take you on the tractor trailer?'

'But Dad, we were so looking forward to it. What's happened to the cliff?' Molly asked.

'I'm not sure exactly. Malcolm told Maggie this morning that he'd received word from the coastguard to say that rocks had been seen falling down the cliff face during a routine coastal check last night, and that it's simply not safe.'

'Coastguard, schmoastguard!' Maria whispered to Pippa, not believing it for a second.

'Oh, no! Can't we get someone out to check it today, Dad? We really want to go down to the beach,' Molly said.

'I'm sorry, darling, and you know how much it

pains me to say no to you both, but it's simply not safe, and I won't be responsible for putting any of you in danger. What would Maggie and Pippa's mothers say if they thought I'd put their girls at risk? I'm sorry, girls but this time it's a no, I'm afraid.'

'OK, Dad, we understand,' Maria said suddenly, surprisingly calm.

'We do?' Molly asked Maria.

'We do!' Maria confirmed. 'Thanks for breakfast everyone. We'll decide about that tractor ride, Dad. Let's go, girls.'

'Maria, have you gone mad?' Molly asked angrily as they headed back. 'I can't believe you've lost your nerve on this one. It was all your idea in the first place!'

'Molly, calm down. I've done nothing of the sort and I resent the accusation!' Maria said.

'OK, sorry. It's just got me so wound up! There's no way our cliff has suddenly developed a falling rock problem. It's too much of a co-incidence. The smugglers must have seen us and panicked. I'd put money on the fact that it's their way of keeping us away from the bay while they get on with the business of . . . of . . . Well, whatever it is they're smuggling!' Molly said, exasperated.

'Exactly right!' Pippa said. 'Didn't you hear what your dad actually said? Malcolm didn't even speak with the coastguard in person. 'The coastguard sent word' – anyone can write a fake note with a fake coastguard's signature!'

'And as for your mum and that discussion about Twinkle howling, I'm more sure than ever now that's connected with what's happening on the beach,' Sally said. 'I heard something similar our first night here, don't you remember? And last time I checked, Condor eggs don't howl, so there's definitely a lot more than egg smuggling going on down there.'

'Oh, my gosh, she's right you know, Mimi. I think it's time to call the police. Let's go back to Dad and tell him everything. I reckon he knows something's up anyway by our reaction this morning.' Molly waited for Maria to answer.

'Maria!' Molly shouted.

'Just one sec, if I don't send this text now, it could ruin my whole plan,' Maria answered.

'Of course she's got a plan!' Pippa, said.

'Maria 'Mastermind' Fitzfoster always has a plan!' Sally squealed with delight.

'Come on then. Let's hear it!' Molly said, giving up on her police idea.

Maria drew a deep breath. 'So . . . today's Friday, right? Or Albie-day, as we've come to know and love it, thanks to Molly's online ordering obsession. I've just texted Albie to see if he can make our drop the last of the day and then take the rest of the afternoon off. If we can't get down to the beach via the cliff steps, we're going to have to approach it from the sea.'

'OK . . . And why do we need to get poor Albie involved in all this?' Molly asked.

'First, we need him to drive us to Barnes Bay, the next one along to ours. How else could we get there without having to ask someone from the house? Mum and Dad wouldn't drop us off at Barnes Bay alone, much less let us hire a boat to go sailing on our own in a million years!' Maria went on.

'Hire a boat? Who's going to hire a boat to us?' Sally said.

'Again, that's where Albie comes in. He's not under age. We'll give him the money, he'll rent the boat and then pick us up further along the bay so no-one knows it's really for us. If the smugglers did see us watching them at any point last night, they have the advantage of knowing who we are, but *we* still have no idea who they are.

'They could be around the boatyard – after all, that blue and white motorboat must be moored somewhere in Barnes Bay. At least if Albie goes alone, he won't raise any suspicion.' Maria said, feeling very pleased with herself and her plan.

'You've thought of flipping everything haven't you, Miss Marple!' Pippa said. 'I wish I had a brain like yours.'

'And I wish I had a singing voice like yours, but our differences are what make us so good when we pull together as a team,' Maria beamed at her friends. 'So, what do you say, gang? Are you with me?'

'Woof!' Twinkle barked, leaping into the middle of them.

'Yes, and you, Twinks! We can't do this without you – you're going to sniff out *egg-sactly* what's going on at Wilton Bay.'

'Woof, woof!' she barked again.

After the girls had finished high-fiving each other, they started to pack their rucksacks.

'Now, try and think of every eventuality!' Maria instructed. 'Who knows what's going to happen on that beach. We need to be as prepared as possible. I've written a list of what I think might be useful, so let's collect everything in a pile on the sofa, and then we'll split it between our bags. The biggest thing is to charge up our walkie-talkie watches.'

Pippa began to read out Maria's list:

4 x torches (2 dim lights)
1 x video camera
1 x stills camera
1 x mini binoculars
Snacks
Water bottle
Flask of hot chocolate
Walkie-talkie watches (fully charged and set to
    channel three)
Compass
Swiss Army Knife
Screwdriver
Hammer

'OK, most of that I get, but a screwdriver and a hammer?' Pippa looked up in surprise. 'I didn't think we were putting together a wardrobe this afternoon.' Sally and Molly smothered a giggle.

'Pips, we've got no idea what the situation is down there. Better to be safe than sorry.' Maria said, undeterred.

Knock, knock.

'Sally, the blanket!' Maria whispered, signalling to Sally to hide their pile of provisions.

'Come in!' Molly called out.

'It's only me,' Maggie said, as she opened the door. 'Not sure what you girls are up to today now, but you've got to eat, so here's lunch and dinner!'

'Thanks, Mum!' Sally said, giving her a bigger hug than usual. 'Love you!'

'Ditto!' Molly agreed.

'My pleasure. Just make sure you keep in touch today over the walkie-talkie watches. I think Mr Fitzfoster's a little concerned you're up to something.'

'Us?' Sally answered. 'Never, Mum.'

Maggie looked doubtful, but she had far too much to do up at the house to get into a discussion about it.

'OK, well, just be safe and have fun. And don't sit in all day watching movies. Get some fresh air in your lungs. It's such a gorgeous day.'

'We will, Maggie. You can count on that!' Maria said with a knowing smile, and Maggie left them to it.

'I love your mum, Sally. Susie, the old housekeeper was adorable but her cooking wasn't a patch on your mum's.'

'Well, it's a good job the Sudburys have taken over then isn't it,' Sally answered happily.

'Do you think we should wear our wellies?' Pippa asked. 'I'm just thinking Albie might not be able to bring the boat right up to the sand, and there will most likely be some wading involved.'

'Good thinking, Pips,' Maria said. 'I was thinking we'd just take our sandals off but your idea's much better. The water's freezing and I hate sandy feet.'

'Wellies on a summer's day . . . What will my followers of fashion think about that? No photos, please!' Molly said in despair, secretly pleased her new wellington boots were quite fabulous.

'Talking of Albie, have you heard back from him yet, Maria?' Pippa asked. 'We're cracking on but the whole plan falls apart without him.'

'Not yet, but he's probably busy with his morning deliveries. It's nearly midday now though, so I'm expecting him to call any minute . . . Or hoping, I should say.'

'One thing you haven't mentioned . . . How on earth are we all going to get down to Barnes Bay? Last time I looked, Albie's motorcycle box would barely even be big enough for Twinkle these days, let alone us as well.'

'You'll see,' Maria said. 'Now are you ready for this, agents. Who knows where we'll be this time tomorrow but I reckon so long as we stick together, we'll be fine!'

'I do hope so – the wedding's in two days and I can't afford to be late!' Pippa said only half-joking.

'Sugar, I'd forgotten all about that! Don't worry, Pips, we'll have you tucked up safe and sound by nightfall,' Molly answered, hoping she was right.

'We sure will. Four heads are better than one, you know,' Sally said, quoting Pippa's song lyric to her.

'Woof!' Twinkle barked indignantly.

'Ohhhhhh! Sorry, Twinks . . . I meant five!'

9

Albie-Day

'Where are we going? I've never taken this route back to the house before,' Sally asked, struggling to keep Twinkle walking by her side, even though she was on a lead.

'We can't risk being seen by Mum and Dad. This way brings you out on the other side of the house, up by the garages,' Molly answered.

Bleep, bleep, sounded Maria's phone.

'It's Albie! He's up for it and he's only half an hour away. I knew we could rely on him. He's always there for us when we're in a scrape.'

'Tell me about it,' Pippa said. 'Without him I'd never have made it back in time to give Lucifette her come-uppance at the Christmas Gala.

'Ah, the good old days,' Molly said fondly. 'Do you know, we haven't once spoken about Lucifette and what she's up to . . . and I've got quite a bit of gossip on her. But that's for another day.'

'What? You can't say that and just stop there!' Pippa said.

'Why don't we save that conversation for our first night back at Garland. We'll probably be in dire need of some gossip by then. Deal?'

'Deal. I guess we've got enough on our plate at the moment,' Pippa said.

'Just for a change,' Molly grinned.

'Right, this is the only bit we've got to sprint across that's visible from the house,' Maria said, pointing over to where the row of garages started.

'Blimey, how many cars have you got?' Pippa asked in astonishment. She hadn't noticed the never-ending row of garages and outbuildings when she'd arrived.

'They haven't all got cars in. Some have got gardening equipment, one's Malcolm and Tom's workshop, and the rickety old stone building at the end is full of logs,' Maria pointed out.

'So which one do we want, and how are we going to get over there without being seen if someone *does* happen to look out of the window,' Sally asked.

'That's a bit of a gamble, but I thought if we radio in and pretend to be checking to let them know we're off for a picnic in the fields after all, it won't matter if we're seen anyway.'

'Good thinking! Go on then, brains,' Molly said.

'FAMILY BEAR, COME IN FAMILY BEAR . . . OVER,' Maria said clearly.

'RECEIVING, BROWN BEAR CUB, WHAT'S THE PLAN THEN? OVER,' came Mr Fitzfoster's deep voice.

'HAVE TAKEN YOUR ADVICE AND ARE OFF FOR A MEADOW PICNIC, PAPA BEAR. MAGGIE'S PACKED US ENOUGH FOOD FOR A MONTH SO IF IT'S ALL RIGHT WITH YOU, WE'LL SKIP SUPPER AND HAVE A MOVIE NIGHT INSTEAD . . . OVER,' Maria said, holding her breath and crossing her fingers for a positive response.

Now we all know telling a fib is wrong, Story-seeker, and Maria hated herself for telling one right now, but this was overridden by the desire to help someone, or something, in need – and she was sure he'd understand later.

'RIGHT-HO, BEAR CUBS, STAY OUT OF TROUBLE . . . OVER.'

The twins couldn't believe their luck.

'We'll still have to check in this evening at some point,' Molly said.

'That's fine – we'll just leave it as late as possible and make sure there's no suspicious background noise to give the game away that we're not actually tucked up in bed!' Maria answered.

'OK. Let's get this show on the road, then!' Molly said.

As the girls scooted across to the other side of the garages, they heard the familiar rumble of a motorcycle coming up the drive.

'Albie!' They all shouted at once and ran to meet him.

'Hiya, L'Etoilettes!' Albie said jumping off his bike and throwing his helmet on the ground. 'How's tricks? I believe we're about to embark on another Fitzfoster special mission?' he said, hugging the girls one by one.

'Indeed!' Maria answered. 'Thanks so much for agreeing to help us, Albie. We knew we could rely on you!'

'Are you kidding? I've been working crazy hours recently, I needed a break and a bit of fun,' Albie said.

'First things first . . . Your delivery m'lady,' he said to Molly, handing her the contents of his bike box.

'Oooooh, exciting. I'll stash these in the garage for the moment and pick them up later. Can't wait!' Molly said matching Albie's smile.

'And I've bought my driver's license, Maria. Are you sure this is going to be all right with your folks?'

'Erm, ask me no questions and I'll tell you no lies,' Maria said wincing.

'Hmmmm, so that's how this is going to go. I'm in, but only because I trust you,' Albie answered.

'Ditto!' Molly said, giving him another hug. 'Right then Maria, what's next?'

'Over here!' she called, pointing a zapper at one of the garages.

The group watched as the garage door rose slowly to reveal an old green Land Rover.

'What a beauty!' Albie said. 'I've always dreamed of going off-road in one of these!'

'Well I can't promise any off-roading today, but there is somewhere we do need to go,' Maria said, scrabbling around on the spare tyre. 'And for that we won't get very far without this!' She held up a shiny key.

'Maria, your knowledge of anything you shouldn't know, never ceases to amaze me!' Molly said, open-mouthed. 'When did you discover that's where the keys are kept?'

'It's called the power of observation, Molly dear. I simply pay attention to everything and everyone at every minute of the day. Poor old Eddie has no idea I know where he puts everything, from the keys to his secret stash of chocolate biscuits!'

'AYKM! None of us are safe from Maria-watch!' Molly joked, rolling her eyes.

'Not even I know what that means,' Maria said, rolling her eyes back.

'Anyone?' Molly asked, looking at her friends. 'AYKM – are you kidding me!'

'Ha! Come on then – let's go!' Sally said, grabbing the key and unlocking the door. The adrenalin had kicked in and she finally felt what she'd missed out on the night of the *Lost Rose* mission.

'Look at her go!' Pippa said. 'Right behind you, Sal!'

And with the girls safely belted up and Twinkle sitting patiently in the boot, peering at them through the grille, Albie put his foot on the accelerator and their adventure began.

10

Barnes Bay

'I reckon we should park behind the post office. There's less chance of the car being seen and recognised there,' Maria said.

'What, here?' Albie asked, pulling in to a one-way street behind the high street.

'Perfect – there are two spaces on the left, which are free parking.'

'Great driving, Albie, by the way. You're a natural!' Pippa said.

Albie blushed the same colour as his head of red hair. 'Aw thanks, Pippa.'

'So where to now, boss?' he asked Maria, pulling to a stop.

'Right, this is where you need to use every theatrical bone in your body. There's a couple of old fishing rods in the boot, which Twinkle's probably sitting on, that you should take to help with your story,' Maria said, as the girls looked on in wonderment.

Maria, Story-seeker, as you know was the queen of detail! No-one had seen her sneak off before breakfast to grab the garage zapper and plant the fishing equipment in the boot!

'My story?' Albie said, closing the boot.

'Yes, as far as anyone you meet is concerned, you're staying with friends and have come to Barnes Bay to rent a boat for a fishing trip,' Maria said.

'I have? And how will I explain you lot, plus poochie here, tagging, along for the ride?' Albie asked, scratching Twinkle's ears.

'We'll be waiting for you to pick us up in the boat further down the beach so that no-one even knows we've left Wilton House. We're not sure the smugglers didn't spot us watching them last night, so we definitely can't take the chance of them seeing us snooping about in Barnes Bay.'

'Smugglers?' Albie said in surprise.

'Maria! What exactly did you tell Albie he was getting involved in today?' Molly said, adamant that Albie should be given all the facts first.

'Don't worry about me, Molly, but thanks for the concern. Maria did say it could be a matter of life and death . . . Which was enough for me. I'm sure I'll pick it up as I go along.'

As the girls accompanied Albie towards the boat yard, they took it in turns to fill him in on the story so far. As a fellow animal lover, he couldn't believe what they were saying and was only too happy to help.

Remember, Story-seeker, that it was Albie who'd originally rescued Twinkle as a puppy.

'Right, this is as far as we go before we start bumping into people,' Maria said.

'Here, I'll take Twinkle,' Sally said, grabbing her lead from Albie.

'One last thing – take my walkie-talkie watch,' Maria said. 'I've turned it to channel three which is the channel we use when we want to talk privately. The girls and I will share the other watches.'

'Wowser!' Albie said, loving a gadget. 'But where

will you guys be waiting – just in case these things don't work from the sea.'

'I promise you'll see us somewhere along the bay – just come out of the boat yard and head along the coast keeping the beach on your left. We'll either spot you and radio you or give you a sign. Got it?' Molly said, giving him some money for the boat.

'Got it!' Albie confirmed. 'See you in about twenty minutes!'

'Good luck!' Molly called after him.

'Who's got the binoculars?' Maria asked, placing her rucksack on the sand. 'Actually, I think they're in your bag, Sally.' The girls had found a deserted old café at the end of the beach to hide behind until Albie got close enough for them to jump aboard.

'Here!' Sally said, handing Maria the binoculars.

'I must be psychic!' Maria said with glee. 'Look, there he is . . . In the little green rowing boat with the white sail. I'm just hoping he's not too far out to sea for the radio to work.'

'Let me try,' Molly said raising her watch to speak. 'COME IN ALBATROSS . . . COME IN . . . ALBA . . .' but she was rudely interrupted by all three of her companions exploding into giggles.

'Albatross?' Pippa asked, her cheeks aching.

'Don't you mean *Albietross*?' said Sally.

'Why not?' Molly snapped and carried on trying to radio the little sailboat. 'We've all got names. Why shouldn't Albie? COME IN ALBIETROSS, ARE YOU RECEIVING . . . OVER.'

'I think you're right, Maria. He's much too far out to pick up our signal. How are we going to get his attention without telling the whole of Barnes Bay we're here at the same time?' Pippa asked.

All of a sudden, Twinkle slipped her lead and the girls watched in amazement as she galloped towards the sea in Albie's direction.

'I don't believe it!' Molly cried.

'I swear Twinkle is a human in doggy clothing sometimes!' Pippa said.

'I know! It's as if she heard every word and is doing her bit to help us!'

As the girls continued to watch, they saw Albie fish a soggy and salty Twinkle out of the waves and onto the sail boat. He only had to look over in the direction she'd come from to spot four little bodies waving madly from the shore.

'Good dog, Twinkle. Clever pup!' he said, patting her dry with his jacket and waving back at the girls.

'Oh, thank goodness he's seen us. He'll get as close as he can and then we'll have to wade the rest of the way,' Maria said. 'Everybody ready?'

'I'm going to give Twinkle the biggest steak for her supper!' Molly said. 'She really is one of us isn't she?'

'Let's hope she's as helpful once we get around to Wilton Bay. That's when we're going to need her,' Pippa said.

The girls watched as Albie anchored the little boat and then quickly waded towards them. As luck would have it their wellies were just about high enough to keep the water out as they went to meet him.

'Here, you girls jump in. I found this pair of fisherman's high waders on board. I can jump in and give us a push out to sea without getting wet,' Albie said, secretly relieved they were back together again.

'How did it go at the boatyard, Albie? Any problems?'

'I don't think so. Plenty of people wandering about, staring at the red-haired stranger in town, but apart from that I think they bought my story. We've got the boat until this time tomorrow. They'd only do twenty-four hour hire,' he said. 'Pretty much cleaned me out of the cash you gave me.'

'I'll bet they did,' Sally said.

'Oh, don't worry about that. You did a brilliant job. So far, so good. Touch wood!' Molly said, grabbing the side of the boat for luck. 'And as for you Miss Twinklet . . . you were fabulous!'

'Woof!' Twinkle barked softly and licked Molly's face.

'So, Captain Albie . . . Or should we call you Albietross?' Pippa said.

Albie looked confused.

'Oh, that was just a code name I came up with for you for use over the radio,' Molly said, feeling slightly embarrassed.

'Albietross! I love it, Moll!' he said.

'OK, then, Albietross . . . to Wilton Bay if you please!'

'Aye, aye!' Albie said and rowed with all his might.

'Thank goodness for that!' Maria said as they rowed around the last rockface to Wilton Bay.

'Thank goodness for what?' Sally asked.

'I know you guys think I'm perfect, but even I

miss things sometimes. We should have had a peek from Dad's bench down to the bay before we left, to check whether the smuggler's boat was anchored here again. Imagine if we'd come around that last rock and crashed straight into them!' Maria said, relieved she could finally say it out loud, now that she knew they were safe.

'I'd prefer to think of you as perfect, Maria, if it's all the same to you' Pippa said, squeezing Maria's shoulder. 'Less for me to worry about that way.'

'There's nothing to worry about, Mimi. We're fine. Surely they wouldn't risk sailing here in broad daylight? Especially not if they think we're on to them,' Molly said.

'Yes, that's what I thought, Moll, but let's not forget, we never actually saw that second person leave the bay last night, did we? Who's to say they're not still there? I'm just saying let's keep our wits about us, eh?' Maria warned.

'I don't know how you girls do it, to be completely honest,' Albie said. 'You seem to have a knack for stumbling on adventures. I reckon you'd find a mystery in a paper bag if you looked hard enough.'

'Thanks, Albie!' Molly said, nearly dropping an oar.

'I think this might be as far as we go,' Albie said, looking towards the shore. 'There's too much weight in this little boat, I don't want us to run aground. I'll let you girls and Twinkle out on those rocks, then I'll throw down anchor a bit further away and wade back to shore.'

Twinkle barked at the mention of her name and before they could stop her, she was back in the salty spray, paddling towards the beach.

'She's going to need a jolly good bath when we get home!' Sally said with a smile.

11

The Secrets of Wilton Bay

'Just take it slowly, Pips. The seaweed on these rocks has made them like an ice rink. Luckily we're in our wellies. We'd have had no grip at all in bare feet,' Maria said, gingerly moving from rock to rock.

'Just a couple more steps . . . There!' Sally said with relief as she jumped onto the sand. 'Well done, team!'

The girls felt they'd earned a sip of pink lemonade as they watched Albie wade out of the sea like some red-headed, Loch Ness monster in his green waders and camouflage jacket.

'So what now, boss?' Albie asked, shedding his waterproofs.

'Right . . . yes . . . Now we cover every inch of this

bay for any signs of life/eggs/smugglers etc,' Maria said looking deadly serious.

'Is that all?' Pippa asked.

'OK, then, let's split into two groups, just in case we run into any trouble, and stay on channel three,' Maria instructed. 'Pippa and Sally, you start at that end of the beach with Albie . . . And Molly, you come with me and Twinkle.'

As they gathered up their belongings, Molly suddenly realised that Twinkle was nowhere to be seen.

'Hold on a sec, guys . . . ' Molly called after Pippa and the others. 'Can you see Twinkle anywhere? She's run off.'

'Oh, my word, she's right,' Pippa said. 'I haven't seen her since she jumped out of the boat and swam ashore.'

'We've all been too engrossed in pink lemonade and Mum's chocolate brownies to notice,' Sally said.

'She can't have gone far – she's probably got her nose in a rock-pool, looking for crabs, which is why she hasn't smelled the brownies,' Maria said, not managing to hide the doubt in her voice.

'TWIN-KLE . . . TWIN-KLE,' they called, cupping their hands to their mouths.

'TWIN-KLE! Here girl!' Molly shouted.

'Over here,' Albie said, suddenly, spotting a trail of doggy footprints in the sand.

'Well done!' Maria cried. 'Why didn't I think of that?! Let's follow them.'

'TWIN-KLE,' Molly called again. 'We're coming, ready or not,' as if it was a game of hide and seek they were playing.

The trail led up the beach to the far end and then came back on itself, almost brushing against the rockface. Every now and again, there was a big scoop out of the sand alongside the foot prints.

'It's as if she kept sniffing for something in the sand,' Pippa said.

'Hot on the trail of our smugglers no doubt,' Molly answered. 'Clever girl.'

'Wait a minute – they've stopped. The prints have just stopped,' Albie said in dismay, looking up at the rockface in front of his nose.

'They can't just stop, unless she's developed the ability to walk through rock or fly back to Hotel L'Etoile in the last twenty minutes. Twinkle - where are you? This isn't funny now,' Molly cried desperately. 'Twin-kle! Twin-kle!'

'Shhhh, Molly, stop!' Maria said throwing her hands

up for silence. There was the faint sound of barking, muffled by the lapping of the waves behind them. 'I can hear her . . .' She stood, listening. 'Can you? Can you guys hear her? It's coming from the other side of this rock. It's as if she's found a way inside the cliff.'

'I can't bear to think about it, she's been caught in a rock-slide or something,' Molly said, tears beginning to roll down her cheeks.

'Molly that's not possible – not without us seeing or hearing it happen. It's windy down here, but not that windy. Look, do you see any rocks anywhere at our feet because I don't? Calm down. We need to think about this . . .' Maria said.

And there it was again, the faint sound of barking, coming from inside the cliff.

'She's one hundred percent inside!' Albie said, feeling his way along the rockface. 'There must be an entrance somewhere. Come on girls, we have to find it. Didn't you say the skinny smuggler just disappeared somewhere on the beach. Well then, this would make perfect sense.'

'You're right, Albie. There must be a crack or crevice of some sort. But I don't see any openings – do you?' Maria scanned the rockface.

'Oh, Twinkle! We're coming – sit tight,' Molly groaned.

Five confused faces stared at the apparently solid stone in front of them. Only Twinkle could manage to find a way into a rock with no opening!

'I don't know what we're going to do if we can't get inside. Suddenly I couldn't give two hoots about our little smuggler problem. If we turn up at L'Etoile on Monday without Twinkle, we'll have a far bigger problem on our hands,' Molly said, slumping onto the sand. 'Can you imagine what Mr Hart will say?'

Suddenly an enormous seagull swooped over their heads, coming in to land on a flat piece of rock above them.

'That's all we need, to get covered in sea-gull poop at a time like this.' Pippa said, glumly.

'They do say it's lucky,' Sally said, trying to cheer everyone up.

'Hold on a second . . .' Maria said with a grin the girls knew only too well. 'That's it! Just ask yourselves if you were Twinkle, what would you be doing if you were standing here right now?' Maria smiled.

'Apart from leaping up onto that ledge after that big ugly seagull you mean? But she's not here, is she

. . . She's stuck insi . . . NW.' Molly stopped in her tracks, realising she'd just given them all the answer.

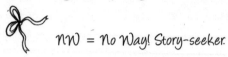

nw = No Way! Story-seeker.

'YW, Molly Fitzfoster!' Maria said.

yw = Yes Way! Story-seeker.

'Quick Albie, give me a hand moving that boulder so we can climb up. It's a bit high for us without it, but Twinkle would have made it onto that ledge no bother.'

And so the five friends used the huge boulder at the foot of the cliff to help them climb onto the ledge. Now, if they'd have had time to think about it, Story-seeker, they'd have realised that such a boulder was rather conveniently placed just where they needed it. Do you think someone had had the same idea before them? Well now, that would be telling wouldn't it?

★ ★ ★

12

Little Dog Lost

'WOW,' Molly said under her breath, staring at the dark, craggy, opening below their feet.

'How have we never found this before?'

They were completely in the cold, damp shadows of the cliff face now.

'Why would you if you weren't looking for it? It's too high up for it to be seen from the beach, and the overhanging rock completely hides it from view from above.' Sally answered.

'Bagsy not going first!' Molly said, a bit creeped out by the big shadowy black hole below. 'Not even a torch is going to show us the bottom it's so dark. Who knows how far down it goes?'

'Well, we didn't climb that high up from the beach to get here, so ground level isn't that far away,' Albie said.

'Unless it's like the world's biggest, widest, dampest, deepest, scariest well!' Molly said.

Maria, for once in her life, also felt a bit nervous. She wasn't great with enclosed spaces at the best of times, and a black hole was definitely the sort of enclosed space she might find tough to deal with.

'Has anyone got anything we can throw down it? We'll be able to tell how deep it is by seeing how long it takes to hit the bottom.' Sally suggested.

'Great idea, Sal!' Maria said, gathering herself and rummaging around in her bag. 'The only thing I've got that's heavy enough for us to hear is the hammer.'

'You knew it'd come in useful for something,' Molly said. 'Go for it!'

And with that, Maria dropped the hammer down into the darkness.

Thud, they heard after only a few seconds.

'What do you reckon?' Maria asked Sally.

'I'm not sure. How fast does a hammer travel?' Sally said, thinking maybe her idea hadn't been as good as she'd first thought.

'It hit the bottom pretty quickly if you ask me. I say we go for it. I don't think we've got many hours left until it's dark, so we'd best get moving,' Pippa said.

'Hold on a sec, there's just one more thing that's nagging me. What if the ground isn't stable? I mean like what if it's quicksand down there? We so should have brought some rope to tie around the waist of whoever goes first to test it out,' Maria said.

'If that's the case then Twinkle wouldn't have made it out either, would she,' Molly said sensibly.

'You're right, Moll,' Maria said. 'What on earth is wrong with my brain today? Of course. Twinkle's proof it's fine down there.'

'Look girls, I'll go first. It's only right,' Albie said, feeling like he should do the gentlemanly thing and lead the way. 'I reckon between you, you can hold onto one of my hands while I lower myself down, just until we know the ground is safe.'

'Let me do it,' Pippa said, unexpectedly brave. 'No offence Albie, but I'm much lighter than you and if anything dodgy happens, I think your strength will be best used to help haul me out, rather than us trying to pull you out to safety.'

'Blimey, Agent Burrows!' Maria said, feeling guilty and impressed by Pippa's bravery. 'Lead the way then.'

As the group helped to lower Pippa, all they could hear were their own hearts beating, interrupted by Twinkle's faint barking.

Pippa's feet finally touched the ground and she kicked around in the darkness. 'It's fine guys, come on down – and fire up those torches!'

The others followed Pippa down into what could only be described as a huge doughnut made of rock, and they were standing right in the centre.

Albie, Pippa and Sally began to have a look around, so Molly seized the opportunity to have a quiet word with Maria.

'Mimi, are you OK. You've not been yourself since we discovered the ledge.'

'I'm not sure. I feel hot and panicky. It's so weird. Maybe I'm coming down with something,' Maria said, wiping her brow.

'I think you're a bit claustrophobic. But you'll be fine. I promise I'll stay by your side. Come on, we need your brains on this one. You can conquer this fear – look at Pippa. One scoot down the cliff and she's a rock climber!'

'Thanks, Moll. I'll be all right in a second,' Maria said. She bent down to pick up the hammer which she'd dropped and put it back in her rucksack.

'There's a huge tunnel this way!' Albie said, calling the others over to him. 'This is unbelievable. I can't work out whether the sea has done this or whether it's man-made. Either way, it's been like this for hundreds of years. Look how smooth these rocks are,' he said, running his hand along the polished stone.

'Oh, my goodness, you're right!' Maria said, her head beginning to clear as she instantly saw the danger they might be in. 'We're going to have to work fast – the tide's going to come in soon, and if the corrosion of this rock is anything to go by, it won't be long before this whole place is entirely under water.'

'Did you just say under water?' Molly said. 'Then we'd better be super-quick! Twinkle! Twinkle! Bark for us so we can find you.'

'Woof, woof, woof,' Twinkle answered back.

'Yes, she's this way,' Pippa said.

So, with Maria taking deep breath after deep breath, the gang followed the tunnel under the cliff in the direction of Twinkle's barking. They couldn't believe how wide it was. OK, the ceiling height made it a bit *crouchy* here and there, but essentially it was a very well excavated route – man-made or otherwise!

'Can you see anything up ahead yet, Pips?' Sally asked, struggling a little. 'Twinkle can't be that far from the beach for us to have heard her.'

'Ouch!' Maria cried suddenly from the back of the group.

'What is it?' Sally stopped. 'Here use my torch.'

As Maria shone the light around her feet she gasped as she saw what she'd stubbed her toe on.

'It's the egg! The Condor's egg!'

'Uh oh!' Sally said. 'I had a feeling we weren't alone in here, but I had hoped it was just Twinkle waiting for us. Now I'm not so sure!'

Albie doubled back to take a closer look. 'Isn't it beautiful,' he said lifting the egg out of the sand. The smugglers must have dropped it and not even realised. 'And wrapping the precious egg in his jumper, he placed it carefully in his rucksack.

'Let's keep going,' Maria said, aware of the time. 'Twinkle must be trapped somewhere or she'd have come and found us by now. We've got to keep going!'

'TWIN-KLE! We're coming,' Molly called again.

'Woof, woof!' came the response.

'She's close! We're close!' Pippa called back to the others and shone her torch around again. 'Yes, over here. It looks like a hatch or something.'

The others caught up with her and they all stared at the huge, round metal door set in the rock.

'That's a water-tight hatch!' Albie said quietly.

'Of course!' Maria agreed. 'Like they have in an airlock chamber on a submarine for transferring between water and air. Blimey, it's just as we feared then, this tunnel must completely flood when the tide comes in.'

'Please stop talking about tides coming in, Mimi. It's TMI,' Molly said. 'I'm not feeling too good to be honest. I don't think there's a whole lot of oxygen in this tunnel as it is.'

TMI = Too much information, Story-seeker

'Don't worry,' Maria said, suddenly feeling stronger now that Molly needed her to be. 'We'll be out of here in no time!'

Pippa took control, while Sally distracted Molly with another swig of pink lemonade.

'How do we get it open then? I can't even see a handle,' Pippa said, feeling around the bolts on the circular door.

'Well it must open or how else did Twinkle get inside?' Sally said.

'The smugglers must not have closed it properly last night in their big hurry to leave the beach.

Twinkle must have nosed it open and then somehow it's slammed shut behind her,' Maria said.

'Mind if I have a go, Pippa?' Albie asked.

'Be my guest!' Pippa said, moving to one side.

As Albie felt around the hatch, he focused less on the bolts and more on the centre of the panel. Suddenly the whole front of it slid forward, revealing a large handle behind.

'Well done, Albie!' Maria gasped.

'What did you do?' Pippa asked.

'I have absolutely no idea. I just leaned on it and the whole front popped off. I'm going to twist this handle right around and hopefully it will open,' Albie said, taking a deep breath. 'Ready?'

'Go!' Maria said, at which point the hatch popped open and a frantic, panting Twinkle leapt right over Albie's head and into Maria's arms.

'Hello, Twinkle!' she said, a relieved tear rolling down her cheek. 'It seems you have a nose for trouble too! Let's go see!'

13

The Smuggler's Hideout

What awaited the five friends and their dog on the other side was nothing less than astounding. It was a cave the size of Wilton House!

'Supercalifragilisticexpialidocious!' Pippa whispered.

'Exactly!' Molly and Maria said together.

'How can this be? What is this place?' Sally said, her eyes like saucers as she took in the rows of cages cut into the walls, all piled on top of each other. 'It's like a zoo with no animals.'

'I'm going to have a quick scout around and check there's no-one here. I'd like to be the one taking them by surprise, rather than the other way around,' Albie said, feeling that as the only boy in the group, he'd better take charge of the girls' safety.

'Thanks, Albie,' Molly said, still clutching Twinkle. 'And you, you little rabbit. Trust you to sniff this place out. You're such a clever girl.'

'Maria, over here!' Pippa called, pointing at one of the cages. There on the floor stood a box like the one they'd seen the skinny smuggler carrying across the beach the night before. The lid was open and all that lay in the bottom were a couple of broken shells.

'Oh, no,' Molly gasped. 'It's like a huge egg box for carrying endangered eggs. And one of them has been broken. This is just horrible.'

Pippa put her arm round Molly's shoulder. 'We're going to stop them, Molly. They won't be able to even look at a bird in the sky from prison, let alone ransack a nest.'

'There's more over here, guys,' Sally called, and they all rushed over to see.

'This is horrendous!' Molly said, as she saw case upon case of the same sort of egg carrier that had upset her so much. 'There must be hundreds of eggs here.'

'Or were . . . My guess is that these old cases have been dumped down here because their contents have already been sold on to illegal collectors. I bet thousands and thousands of pounds have changed hands for these eggs,' Sally said.

'You're not wrong!' Maria shouted over. 'Look at this!'

Maria had found a large table, covered with packing boxes, tape and various tools. 'I found this underneath the junk. It's some sort of log book. I think it holds the key to every egg and goodness knows what else has been smuggled through Wilton Bay through the years. It's all in code though.'

'Well done, Mimi! That's exactly the sort of evidence we need to hand over to the police. Put it in your bag and let's get out of here. This place is giving me the creeps. We've done what we came to do, pleeeeease can we let the police do the rest? They'll have to believe us when they see that book,' Molly said, clipping on Twinkle's lead.

Maria looked serious for a moment.

'Guys, look. I know you want to go back. And believe me, I've been struggling with a major attack of claustrophobia since we jumped into the doughnut, but we're here now, and we've got one shot at finding out as much as we can about what exactly has been going on down here. I think we're safe with the tide for another hour, so what do you say? Another twenty minutes?'

Molly looked at Pippa and Sally who looked as unsure as she did.

'Shall we put it to a vote?' Pippa said. 'All those in favour of leaving now, hands up.'

Molly's hand twitched. She was desperate to go home, but she had to support Maria.

Only Sally put her hand up. 'I don't know guys, this place is horrible. Look at the hairs on my arm . . .' she said, rolling up her sleeve. 'The hairs have been standing on end like that since we came in here. Please can we go?'

Pippa continued with the vote. 'All those in favour of another twenty minutes and then straight home?'

Albie, Maria, Molly and Pippa's hands went up.

'Sally, just a little bit longer, OK? We'll look after you. It'll be fine, I promise!' Maria said.

Sally reluctantly agreed and looked after Twinkle as the others busied themselves searching for goodness knows what.

It truly was the most bizarre place, Storys-seeker, not to mention completely Creepsville!

'Um, I think you'd better come and see this, girls,' Albie said, climbing out of one of the larger cages. His face was even paler than usual against his mop of red hair.

'Albie! Where did you come from?' Molly said, shocked.

'That's just it, Molly, this isn't just another cage. It's the entrance to a whole new set of problems.'

Maria's ears pricked up from the other side of the cave and she was over in a second. Albie carried on. 'While I was having a poke around, I noticed a strip of light on the floor against the back wall of this cage and I got to thinking – there's no light on in there, so it must be coming from behind. So I went in and gave the wall a shove and . . .'

'Show us, Albie!' Maria said. And there, just as he had described, was another exit at the back of the cage. 'And that's where I found these poor little guys . . .' he said, nodding towards some of the saddest, furry faces the girls had ever seen.

As they entered the second room, they saw more cages, but this time, each cage had an occupant.

'Oooooowwww!' came a growly howl from the first cage.

Sally rushed over and saw a forlorn looking Grey

Wolf cub, with his nose in the air.

'Oh, no, this is terrible!' she cried, moving along the cages, clutching her nose from the smell.

'There's a little Orangutan over here!' Molly gasped.

'Grrrrrrrrrr . . .' came a baby roar from the far corner.

'Don't tell me that's what I think it is!' Molly said to Albie, who was staring through the bars.

'If you're thinking orange with black stripes, I'm afraid you're right, Molly.'

'There's a whole zoo of exotic animals here,' Molly said.

'And these are just the ones here at the moment. Who knows how many other poor animals have been kept here,' Pippa replied.

'We've got to do something!' Molly said holding her watch up in a panic. 'COME IN PAPA BEAR . . . PAPA BEAR . . . ARE YOU THERE PAPA BEAR?'

'Moll, we're never going to get any signal – we don't know how deep down we are, or even where we are. We've got to get out of here, right now,' Maria said decisively.

'But I can't leave these poor animals, Mimi. They're going to die if we don't help them,' Molly said.

'Maria's right, Molly. This is far worse than we could ever have imagined, but there's nothing we can do to help them from in here. We've got to get back to the boat and radio for help,' Albie said, calmly.

'Quick, everyone grab your stuff! To the hatch.'

'Don't worry, guys,' Molly whispered to the miserable faces in the cages. 'We're going to get help… just a little longer…OK?'

She turned and headed back to join the others in the main cave.

'WAIT! Shhhhhh!' Maria shouted as they opened the watertight hatch.

The others were silent.

'Do you hear that?' she whispered. Everyone held their breath to listen.

'Jeepers, it's water!' Sally said in alarm. 'Look!'

As they looked on the water, which they'd first heard as a trickle in the darkness, suddenly started to curl towards them through the tunnel, lapping at the cave walls. It was unstoppable and rising.

'Hurry! Back into the cave - we've got to shut this door. We're too late to get out this way. The tide's coming in!' Maria cried.

'What? How long have we been in here?' Molly whimpered. 'I told you we should have left earlier, Mimi.'

'I know that now!' Maria snapped. 'I'm sorry, guys, OK. I made a mistake. The tide's not due in for at least another hour. Albie are you sure that's locked tight?'

Albie turned and nodded. 'At least we know it is water-tight. The fact that our new friends in the other cave are still breathing tells us that.'

'Oh, Albie don't!' Pippa said. 'How on earth are we going to get out of here now? What if the smugglers come back tonight when the tides gone out and it's dark.'

'You'd have thought they would have put a spyhole in that hatch so you could see when the tide has gone out again, wouldn't you?' Maria said, more frustrated than ever.

'They wouldn't need to – they'd be prepared and know things like tidal schedules. We, on the other hand, are stuck completely between a rock and a hard place . . . 'scuse the pun!' Sally said, not even trying to be funny.

'Oh, Mimi, I'm frightened,' Molly said, and Maria's face fell.

'I'm so sorry, guys, I just didn't expect this. We

all knew it was risky, but I take full responsibility for dragging you here. And now we're stuck. I'm so sorry.' And for the first time in a long time, Maria put her head in her hands, a secret tear rolling down her cheek.

Somehow, Maria's unexpected despair boosted the rest of the group. They'd never seen her without a plan and all felt they wanted to protect her from feeling helpless.

'Mimi, you can't give up now. Come on, think!' Molly said, trying to snap her sister out of it. 'We need your brain now more than ever.'

Maria looked up. 'I hate to say it guys, but I'm fresh out of ideas. We're just going to have to await our fate, whatever that might be.'

'Nonsense!' Pippa said, taking off her rucksack. 'Let's think. You said yourself only yesterday there could be another way out of this bay – one that only the smugglers know about. How else would the skinny smuggler have got out?'

'Right! We know he didn't get in the boat with Big Smuggler. And he's definitely not in here, so where's he gone?' Sally said. 'There must be another way out.'

'I know you're trying to be positive, Pippa, but Big Smuggler could have rowed back to collect Skinny

Smuggler later at night, when he thought the coast was clear. Let's face it, I've really screwed up this time!' Maria answered, throwing her hands up again, to cover her eyes.

Molly stared at Pippa in alarm. She'd never ever seen her sister like this before and it scared her.

'Actually, Maria, what Pippa and Sally are saying, makes sense,' Albie said.

Maria looked at him, a glimmer of hope in her eyes.

'I mean, they might get these animals into the bay by boat, but they can hardly store them here, then put them back on a boat to Barnes Bay and offload them there can they? They'd be seen or heard.'

The girls were all nodding, their minds alive with possibilities.

'Wilton Bay is being used for more than just storage, and that's because it's completely secluded. As is your house and the land around it. I don't care what you say, there simply must be some way out to the cliff top where these animals are being loaded into a lorry and shipped off around the country.'

'Albietross – you genius you!' Maria exclaimed. 'He's right, girls, he's totally right!!'

'That's a relief, I've never been so terrified,' Pippa said.

'What of being stuck down here? I know,' Maria asked, guiltily.

'Not that, silly! Seeing you give up on a problem without solving it! Don't ever do that again Agent Fitzfoster!' Pippa told her.

'I won't, I promise,' Maria said.

'Right, team, get hunting – but don't go back into the animal cave unless you have to. I don't think it's fair to tease them by going in without any food,' Albie said.

Thank goodness for Albietross . . . Or that should that be Captain Albietross?

14

The Only Way is Up

'I have to admit, I'm getting a bit worried,' Albie said. 'We've been searching for a way out for hours and still nothing!'

'I won't hear of it – not from you, Captain. What you said was absolutely right, and I refuse to believe we're not going to be back at Hotel L'Etoile, watching movies and munching popcorn before the night's out,' Maria said positively.

'I jolly well hope so, or Dad'll be sending out a search party. I've just realised we completely forgot to radio in to say goodnight before entering this cave. He'll be furious with us,' Molly said.

'Oh, sugar – you're right. Blast! I can't believe I

forgot that before we jumped into the doughnut of darkness!' Maria groaned.

'Look, don't worry. It's only just dinner time,' Sally said, checking her watch. 'How far do you suppose we are from the house?' Sally asked.

'Not sure, the tunnel seems to go on and on, but everything is exaggerated in the dark. For all we know, we're right underneath Hotel L'Etoile!' Pippa said, feeling comforted by that thought.

'Twinkle – what do you think?' Molly asked, stroking the dog's silky ears. 'You're Princess Mystery-Solver. Any ideas?'

But Twinkle was exhausted. All the excitement had clearly been too much for her. She'd barely moved from a pile of rugs she'd been lying on since they'd closed the hatch.

'Oh, Twinks, here have a biscuit,' Sally said, popping a dog biscuit that her mother had thoughtfully packed into Twinkle's mouth.

The biscuit seemed to give her a burst of energy, and even before she'd swallowed it she sprang up with a *woof,* scattering rugs left, right and centre.

'Ha! Glad to see you're feeling better, Twinkle! Now all you have to do is find us a way out of here,' Pippa said.

'Woof!' Twinkle barked as if to say, 'OK, then' and she scampered off to sniff around the cages.

'Ah poor thing – she must be so confused by all these random animal smells. It only smells damp and musty to us in here, but imagine what it's like for her,' Maria said.

'Do you think she'd go barking mad if we took her into the animal room? We've searched the rest of this cave high and low for a way out. If there's not an escape route in that room then I think it's safe to say we're trapped!' Albie said, frowning.

'Shall we try it? I know you didn't want us to disturb those poor baby animals any more than we have to, but I think we have to check, Mimi, don't you?' Molly said.

'OK, well let's have a quick tidy up in here and try and leave things as we found them, just in case we don't come back this way,' Maria said, always one step ahead.

Well most of the time, Story-seeker. On this occasion, she was what is known as temporarily stumped!

♡

They tiptoed through the cage entrance to the secret animal cave. As luck would have it, both the wolf and tiger cubs were sleeping, but the orangutan was wide awake and rushed to the front of the cage as they walked by.

'Not long now, little one,' Maria said softly. 'We're going to get help I promise.'

'Can you see anything, Albie?' Molly whispered to Albie who was leading the way.

'Not a single thing. These cages run almost the full length of this back wall, so there's no way out there, nor can I see any openings anywhere else. Grrrrr! This is so frustrating!' Albie grumbled.

'We're close, I can feel it,' Sally said. 'In actual fact – I can really feel it.'

'Feel what?' Pippa dived over to Sally's side. 'A draught – I can feel a draught and seeing as there are no windows to the beach here, there must be an opening somewhere.'

'She's right guys – come over here. There's a really cold breeze coming this way from behind the orangutan's cage,' Pippa said.

'Sorry little guy,' Albie said as he shone his torch through the bars at the back of the cage. 'Now this is funny. Why would the cages need bars at the back if there was solid wall behind?'

'Bingo, Albie!' Maria said suddenly. 'Because it's not a solid wall at all! Look! Point the torch up there . . .'

And as Albie moved the circle of light across the back of the cage it was like the rock behind was moving in the breeze.

'That's it! That's where the draft is coming from. Quick guys – let's get behind these cages. It's not a wall at all, it's a black curtain!' Maria said.

Maria ran to the end of the row of cages and ducked around the back. She grabbed the edge of the curtain and dragged it back as far as it would go.

'AYKM?' Molly gasped.

AYKM = Are you kidding me,
remember from earlier Story-seeker?

'Are you guys seeing this?' Maria said, as the rest of them joined her. 'Can this place get any crazier?'

There before them was a sort of train platform, complete with three huge open-top trailer-type railcars. And, at their feet, the start of a railway track which lead away into the darkness ahead.

'I just don't believe what I'm seeing!' Molly said, nearly dropping Twinkle's lead.

'But where on earth do these tracks go to?' Pippa said. 'How do we know we're not going to bump straight into the very people we've been trying to avoid?'

'I don't think we have any other option. My feeling is we'll come out somewhere on Wilton land, but as for who'll be waiting for us the other end, your guess is as good as mine,' Maria said.

'Albie! Be careful!' Sally called out as Albie darted over to the first carriage.

'No time to waste, girls. This is definitely it. Our ticket out of here. The quicker we get out, the quicker we can get help for the animals. I just need to work out how we get these cars moving,' Albie said, circling the first car. 'Mind you, I've a horrible feeling it's not connected to any electricity – hope you girls are feeling strong!'

'Wowser! It's going to be a long way up to the top, wherever that is, without any power. We'd best have a sugar fix now to keep our energy up!' Sally said, handing out the last of her mum's brownies.

'Oh, my goodness! I had no idea how much I needed that,' Molly said, savouring every bite.

Sometimes, Story-seeker, in moments of immense stress and pressure, only chocolate will see you through!

'Guys, I need a hand over here. I think we should start by lifting one of these cars onto the track. At least then we can have a proper look at how we get it moving,' Albie said.

The girls were at his side like a shot, leaving Twinkle munching biscuits and keeping watch.

'Ready, steady, heeeave!' Albie instructed, and they managed to shift the huge car over the platform and into position on the track in one smooth movement.

'Wow, girls! You made light work of that. I don't think a bunch of chaps could have done a better job!' he said.

'I can guarantee you they wouldn't!' Maria said, slightly annoyed by the comparison.

'CO, Mimi. The Captain's only joking with you, aren't you Albie?' Molly said.

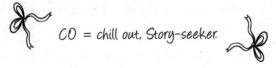

CO = chill out, Story-seeker.

'Um . . . yep . . . yep . . . Just kidding,' Albie said, backtracking.

'Now what?' Sally asked, staring at the rail car. 'There aren't any buttons, no steering wheel, no fuel tank, no . . . No nothing as far as I can see. It's just a big wooden box on wheels.'

'Maybe the smugglers use the ruts on the track like a staircase and push the cars up to the top,' Molly said, puzzled.

'Hang on a sec,' Albie said, pressing down on a pedal he'd found on the floor of the car. 'This is a foot-brake! I've seen this before . . . I know exactly what this is, he continued, jigging about. 'But there's a bit missing. Can anyone see a wooden T-shaped bar anywhere?'

The girls scurried around the platform, their torches casting spooky shadows.

'Nothing over here,' Sally called from the left, nearly jumping out of her skin when she felt Twinkle's wet nose nudging her pocket for more goodies.

'Nor here,' Pippa said from the right.

'What about underneath either of the other two cars? Maybe the smugglers hid it, just in case someone who shouldn't be here, got this far and tried to use their escape route,' Albie said.

'Ha! Well, they didn't gamble on five genius detectives like us, did they?' Maria said triumphantly, as she emerged from under the second car, dragging an enormous T-shaped bar. 'Will this do?'

'That's it!' Albie said jumping up and down. 'Now if only we had a screwdriver so that I can bolt this thing together.'

Pippa looked at Sally, who looked at Molly, who looked at Maria, who gave them her smuggest *I told you so* face.

'Seeing as there aren't any wardrobes to put up down here, Pips, perhaps you'd be good enough to pass these handy tools to Captain Albietross,' Maria said, handing the screwdriver and hammer to Pippa.

Well, we always knew she'd be justified in packing those tools in the end, didn't we, Story-seeker?

'OK, OK, OK! I admit it – you are the genius and we are mere students in the presence of your greatness, oh Brilliant One,' Pippa said, pretending to bow.

'Just so long as you realise that, we're cool!' Maria said, giggling as Albie busied away inside the car.

'I just can't believe that there's a tunnel running through this cliff, big enough to fit such a huge car through. Can you imagine the nightmare someone had back in the day, carving this?' Molly said.

'I know. And it must be like this all the way up to the top,' Pippa replied.

'Albie – you're so clever, working out that this is a handcar,' Maria said, full of admiration for Albie's practicality and skill.

'I don't like the sound of that!' Molly said. 'What's a handcar when it's at home? Where's the key?'

'Well . . .' Maria said, loving a question that started with the words what, when or how. 'There's no key I'm afraid. That T-Bar thing looks like junk, but it's actually an arm which pivots like a seesaw when you connect it to the base of the car. Once it's fixed in place, you pump it up and down and in turn it moves the wheels along the track underneath.'

'Maria, you literally are a human encyclopedia!' Sally said.

'I can't take the credit this time, girls. This is all Albie's brain power,' Maria admitted.

'There!' Albie said, tightening the last bolt and passing the screwdriver back to Maria. 'That should do it!'

'Well done, Albie! I reckon we should have two people either side and one standing at the back with their foot above the brake in case we run into any trouble!' Maria said.

'Good thinking,' Albie agreed. 'Come on then smuggler-hunters! What are you waiting for? Let's get out of here, before we join the long list of endangered species!'

None of them needed to be told twice, and within seconds, the five friends and their dog were poised for action.

15

The Great Escape

'*P*ush!' Albie called out.

'Pull!' Maria shouted back.

'Push!' Albie called again

'Pull!' Maria answered until, on either side of the T-bar, they were pumping in a perfect rhythm.

'It's working!' Molly squealed with delight as the car started to move up the track.

Molly, along with Twinkle, was in charge of the brake pedal. She was relieved, but more than happy, to swap with one of the others half-way up if their arms got tired. Albie had teamed up with Sally on one side of the car and Maria was on the other with Pippa.

'We've . . . just . . . got . . . to . . . keep . . . up . . .

the . . . rhythm . . . so . . . we . . . keep . . . moving,' Maria said in time with pulling up the bar.

'She's right, guys,' Molly said. 'If you stop or slow, it'll be a nightmare to get going again – especially now it's starting to get steeper. We've no idea how strong this brake is, and I for one don't fancy rolling backwards down to the cave.'

'Well you . . . for one . . . have quite a lot . . . to say . . . for a . . . spectator!' Maria said, her arms beginning to ache already.

'Sorry, sis, you're all doing brilliantly,' Molly said, realising she had better keep quiet and focus on trying to light up the track ahead.

'Wow, this is . . . getting tougher . . . it's soooo steep,' Pippa huffed and puffed, too scared to let go of the bar for even a second to mop her brow.

Suddenly, and just as they thought it couldn't possibly get any tougher, the front of the car rose significantly, tipping them all back and making it even harder to pump the bar.

'Keep moving guys! Don't stop!' Molly said in a panic.

'We're definitely . . . climbing now,' Albie panted. 'How many metres down . . . do you reckon we were . . . when Molly tried . . . to radio your dad?'

'Over a hundred . . .' Maria said pumping away. 'But we must be more . . . than half way now . . .'

'How can you tell?' Molly asked in astonishment.

'The colour of the rock . . . it's changed since we started . . .' Maria answered, as though everyone should know about rock formation and its various layers.

Molly smiled at her ever clever twin. 'Exactly! Come on guys. I'm happy to swap if you're tired,' she offered, knowing full well no-one would dare risk losing momentum.

'Aaaaaaaarrrrghh!' They screamed and jumped as the car hit a huge bump in the track.

'What was that?' Sally screeched, worrying that Twinkle might have jumped out or something.

'It's OK,' Molly said calmly, hanging over the back of the car with her torch to see what they'd hit. 'These tracks are rickety that's all. There was a bit of a gap in the rails.'

Secretly, Molly gulped with relief. Her version to the others of *a bit of a gap* was about a metre of track on one side. She had no idea how the car had managed to get over it. She crossed her fingers that there would be no more situations like that and turned to face the front.

'We're nearly there, guys. I can feel it, can't you?' Molly said, trying to keep their spirits up.

'I can't . . . feel much . . . of anything . . .' Sally muttered, breathless. 'Least of all . . . my arms.'

Molly felt helpless. She was desperate to take over and give Sally a rest. She honestly looked as if she was about to pass out in a sweaty heap.

'Sally, just think how beautiful your toned arms will look in the new dress I ordered you, and that Albie brought with him,' she said.

'New dress?' Sally said, suddenly finding a burst of energy.

Molly nodded frantically, seeing she'd touched a good nerve.

'And you, Pips,' she promised. 'You're going to look like a goddess at that wedding on Sunday! Just a few more metres . . .'

Suddenly, just as Molly had predicted, the gradient levelled so they were no longer climbing, only to tip forwards and shoot downhill, forcing them all to let go of the T-bar and grab the sides for dear life. Even Twinkle jumped up to see what was going on.

'Wooooooooooooohooooooo!' Albie shouted with joy as the car raced along, his red hair blowing madly in the breeze.

'Uh-mazing!' Maria squealed, enjoying the blast of fresh air hitting her hot face.

As the track began to even out, the car started to slow and eventually came to a complete stop. For a few seconds everyone was silent, catching their breath and trying to compute the experience they'd shared.

'I've got to give it to you girls, you sure know how to party!' Albie said, throwing his head back and laughing.

And the others joined in. It was laughter borne out of the relief and happiness they felt just to have got this far in their escape from the smuggler's cave.

16

The Great Escape....Continued...

Twinkle was first out of the car, leaping over the side to the platform.

'Woof!' she said happily, waiting for the others to catch up.

'I think she just told us to hurry up!' Molly said. 'We're coming.'

'Molly, can you help me put my rucksack on – my arms are like lead!' Sally said, trying hopelessly to pull it on.

'And me!' Pippa said, trying to shake some life back into her muscles. 'I don't think any of us will be able to move tomorrow. How on earth am I going to hold a microphone to sing in the church on Sunday?'

'We'll get you a stand, and at the worst it'll be the most glamorous mic stand you've ever seen!' Molly said, helping Pippa on with her bag.

As the girls clambered onto the platform, and Maria sat staring at yet another hatch up ahead working out their next move, Albie stared back at the railcar, wondering what had just happened and the trail they'd left behind.

Quickly, he jumped onto the tracks and pushed the car forwards to where there were two more hidden under dust sheets. He carefully spread the dustsheet over all three cars and stood back to see whether three were noticeable. Not really. Well not immediately, anyway. He just hoped the smugglers wouldn't remember that there had originally been three cars in the animal cave and only two up here.

Mind you, Story-seeker, that was the least of their worries. Of course the smugglers would soon know that someone had been in their cave. The best thing team Fitzfoster could hope for now was that the smugglers would be too greedy to abandon the animals in the cave and that they'd once again use that secret railway to get them out so that they could get their money's worth. That's how they could be *caught in the act! But let's just forget about that for a moment – we're getting well ahead of ourselves, Story-seeker. Back to the hatch at the end of the platform!*

'Am I the only one wondering where on earth this is going to bring us out?' Maria said, looking at their only way out at the end of the platform.

'Who knows? It must be dark by now, so we can creep out without being seen,' Albie said.

'Mimi, please, for once in your life, can you just have a little faith and optimism? I've got a feeling we're going to be fine. We've survived against the odds this far without getting caught,

'Touch wood!' Sally said, moving her jelly-like arms to pat the wooden hatch for luck. 'Let's get on with it then, shall we? Who wants to do the honours?' she continued, nodding towards the large metal bolt across the hatch. 'Albie? I reckon you deserve it most, for getting us up here in the first place.'

'Yes, go for it Captain! I don't know what we'd have done without you today,' Molly said.

'A flipping brilliant team effort! That's what I'd call it!' Albie blushed as he grabbed the bolt and loosened it.

He reached forwards and flung the hatch open, keeping his head out of sight until he'd had a chance to check they couldn't be seen. Immediately the platform was flooded with moonlight, and the smell of freshly cut grass engulfed them.

They all took in a deep breath, filling their lungs with fresh, clean air, not realising how thick and damp the air had been inside the rock.

'Mmmmmm . . . My two favourite smells . . . Cut grass and Christmas trees!' Molly said breathing deeply. 'It's like sinking into a bath with your favourite book,' Molly said dreamily.

'I know exactly what you mean . . .' Pippa said, her eyes closed, basking in the moonlight.

'And thanks to your overactive nose, Molly, I know exactly where we are without even having to go outside!' Maria said, suddenly, climbing over Albie to check whether she was right.

'Come on you guys! The coast is clear and you'll never guess where we are!' she said, popping her head back in the hatch to hurry the others.

'I don't believe it!' Pippa said as she emerged. 'We're practically back where we started!'

And they were! The hatch had brought them up behind the furthest and oldest garage in the row, the one where the winter fuel was kept. The one place, none of the Fitzfoster family would have cause to go to, other than to grab a few logs for winter fires.

'But how did you know, Mimi?' Molly asked. 'How could you tell where we were without even looking?'

'It was all thanks to you. You and your talk of Christmas trees. The smell of cut grass could have been anywhere. Malcolm was zooming around on the lawnmower this morning, but as soon as you said Christmas trees, I knew we had to be by the log house. Don't you remember when all those pine trees fell down in that storm last year? I remember seeing trailer load after trailer load of pine logs going past the sitting room window as they cleared them away. There's only one place at Wilton that would smell like Christmas trees in the summer time, Molly, and you hit the nail on the head!'

'Genius, Maria, honestly. I don't know what to say,' Pippa said, shaking her head.

'I haven't finished yet. Quiet everyone – I need to radio Dad and quick!' Maria said checking her walkie-talkie watch. It was worse than she thought – ten o'clock. She was surprised the place wasn't teeming with police looking for them.

'PAPA B . . .' she began.

'MARIA! WHERE HAVE YOU BEEN? ARE YOU ALL RIGHT?' came Brian Fitzfoster's angry voice. 'YOUR MUM AND I WERE ABOUT TO CALL THE POLICE!'

'PAPA BEAR I'M SO SORRY – WE'VE BEEN OUT ALL DAY AND HADN'T NOTICED THAT OUR WALKIE TALKIE BATTERIES HAD GONE FLAT.'

'GET TO BED ALL OF YOU AND WE'LL SPEAK ABOUT THIS IN THE MORNING.'

'YES, DAD,' Maria said, sounding devastated.

'AND MARIA?'

'YES, DAD?' Maria answered nervously.

'I WANT YOU TO TEXT ME A PHOTO OF YOU ALL TUCKED UP IN BED WITHIN THE NEXT FIVE MINUTES – IS THAT CLEAR?'

'YES, DAD,' Maria answered. 'NIGHT, NIGHT.'

'GOOD NIGHT, GIRLS ... OVER.' And with that the radios went quiet.

'We're for it in the morning,' Molly said.

'Well, don't worry about that now. We've got bigger things to think about, like how we're going to rescue those poor babies from that cave!' said Maria.

'Plus the fact that we've only got three minutes to send a photo of us tucked up in bed!' said Sally.

'Quick, let's go. Pyjamas, photo, then we can drink our body weight in hot chocolate while we work out what to do about those poor animals in the cave,' Molly said, whistling gently for Twinkle to join her.

'You girls go ahead. I need to tie up a couple of loose ends,

'What loose ends?' asked Molly. 'You can't leave. We need your input on what to do next, Captain.'

'I need to get the boat. We can't just leave it moored in your bay. That'll set off alarm bells with the smugglers, your family and my family come to think of it. They'll track me down here and think I've drowned or something!' Albie explained.

'He's right, you know,' Pippa said 'Good thinking. But how will you get to it? We left the car, and even if you manage the hike down to Barnes Bay, you can't swim all the way around to the boat.'

'I'll think of something,' he said, scratching his head.

'You can take the cliff steps!' Molly said. 'I'm ninety-nine percent sure there's nothing wrong with them. That was just a ruse to keep us away from the bay.'

'Cliff steps?' Albie asked, intrigued, and the girls explained everything to him on the way to Hotel L'Etoile.

'Right…and send!' Maria texted her dad the sleepiest picture she and her fellow smuggler detectives could muster.

'Poor Albie. I can't believe he's gone straight off like that. Mind you, I'm glad he went that way now. At least he'll be able to spot if the smugglers are back from the viewing platform, before they can see him,' Pippa said as she slurped the last of her cocoa.

'Isn't he just the best?' Molly agreed. 'He must be as exhausted as we are. How he's going to use his arms to row back to the bay and then drive back to the house, I have no idea. And then he's got to take the bike back to London. He must be crazy!'

'Couldn't you have convinced him to stay the night and leave early in the morning?' Pippa said.

'Do you think we didn't try? It was no use. He's got to be back at work and ready to make his Saturday deliveries by seven o'clock tomorrow morning,' Maria answered.

'Gosh, no rest for Captain Albietross, eh!' Sally said. 'Fingers crossed for him.'

'He'll be fine, Sal. He's promised to text us when he's dropped the car back and before he leaves for London, so we don't worry. He could have scaled the steps and rowed round to Barnes Bay in about forty-five minutes . . . Then I reckon another fifteen to collect the Land Rover and get back here,' Maria said. 'Which by my watch means he should be arriving about now.'

After half an hour passed, there was still no word from Albie. Nor was his phone switched on which probably meant it was still at the bottom of his bike box.

'I'm getting worried,' Molly said suddenly. 'Mimi, this doesn't feel right. I say we don't wait for Albie but go and speak to Dad this very minute. I know he's already furious with us but this could be a matter of life and death!'

'Molly just give me five minutes. As we speak, I'm typing up a report of everything that's happened for Dad to hand to the police. I just want to get it all down before we go and see him. You know what he's like. He'll be furious with us at first and not listen to a single thing we say, so at least if we hand him something he can read, we might have a better chance of getting our point across.

'OK, but hurry. We're going to be in trouble whatever we do, but I just can't shake this feeling that Albie's in even more trouble. And even if he's not, those animals sure are,' Molly said, her face showing the strain of the last few hours.

'I tell you what, why don't you and Sally run over to the garages and see if the Land Rover's back and Albie's bike gone? It might just be that his phone is out of battery so he can't text,' Maria said, without looking up from her screen. 'Then Pippa and I will meet you by the kitchen door.'

'And then we'll tell Dad?' Molly said desperately.

'And then we'll tell Dad everything,' Maria agreed. 'In the next hour, the police will be on the doorstep reviewing this log book we brought back with us and be off to arrest the smugglers. I promise. Now go!'

Maria and Sally threw on their coats and were out of the door in seconds.

'You don't think she's right, do you, Pips?' Maria said nervously, zipping the log book into her jacket pocket.

'Oh, no, you're doing that thing again!' Pippa said.

'What thing, Pips?' Maria answered.

'That thing you did earlier when I realised you don't always have all the answers,' Pippa said, frowning.

'Oh, Pippa, I'm not perfect and you're the only one I can share my worries with. Molly always looks to me for answers and I can't bear to let her down. Are you asking me to pretend with you too?' Maria said.

'Not for a second!' Pippa replied, touched that Maria should trust her so much.

'OK, good! I need to know I can always be honest with you, Pips. Right that's finished! Just set this to print and we can go,' Maria said, switching on the little wireless printer. 'Still no word from Albie,' she continued, glancing at her phone.

'You don't think . . .' Pippa hesitated. 'You don't think the smugglers caught him on the beach do you?'

'Anything's possible, Pippa,' Maria said. 'Use your watch to radio Molly and see if the Land Rover's back in the garage.

'PINK BEAR CUB, PINK BEAR CUB . . . COME IN . . . THIS IS YELLOW BEAR CUB. ANY SIGN OF THE CAR OR BIKE . . . OVER,' Pippa said, shouting into her watch.

'ROGER YELLOW BEAR CUB . . . JUST OPENING THE GARAGE NOW . . . HOLD ON . . . OVER . . . '

Pippa crossed her fingers.

'IT'S NOT HERE, MIMI, IT'S NOT HERE!' Molly said forgetting to use any walkie-talkie talk.

Maria rolled her eyes. 'CLARIFICATION NEEDED ... WHAT'S NOT THERE, MOLLY? THE CAR OR THE BIKE ... OVER.'

'THE CAR, MIMI. THE CAR'S MISSING AND HIS BIKE'S STILL HERE, EXACTLY WHERE HE LEFT IT. HE'S NOT BACK! ALBIE'S NOT BACK!'

'ON OUR WAY, BEAR CUBS. MEET YOU AT THE RENDEZVOUS IN ONE MINUTE. OVER ...'

And as Maria and Pippa headed to the front door, another voice came over the walkie-talkie ... A voice they knew and loved, but at this moment felt absolutely terrified of!

'AND WHERE MIGHT THIS RENDEZ-VOUS BE, BEARCUBS? YOU ARE ALL TO COME DIRECTLY TO MY STUDY – RIGHT NOW!' said a furious Mr Fitzfoster over the radio.

'Uh-oh!' Molly and Maria said, even though they were in completely different places.

'Pippa!' Maria cried. Tell me your watch is on channel three!'

Pippa looked down and then up again in horror. 'Erm . . . it's on channel seven. Your dad's heard the whole thing. Oh, Maria, I'm so sorry,' she said, tears forming in her tired eyes.

'Oh, don't worry, Pips. It was me who switched to channel seven when I checked in with Dad. I should have reminded you to switch it to channel three just now. Sugar!'

'Maria! I feel so stupid. And I've been so careful up until now too. I just never thought they wouldn't still be on channel three. That's you being too thoughtful Mimi, and me being totally thoughtless!' Pippa scolded herself and began to cry.

'Look don't worry – it was bound to happen at some point, and we're off to tell Dad everything anyway. In a funny way, maybe he'll have chance to calm down between now and us getting to the study.' Maria said, giving Pippa a squeeze. 'Talking of which . . . we'd better get a move on!'

17

To Catch a Smuggler

*B*y the time the four girls and Twinkle had let themselves in through the kitchen door and headed for the only room in the house with a light on, Mr Fitzfoster had been pacing the floor for almost ten minutes.

'Oh, thank goodness you're all all right!' Linda Fitzfoster exclaimed, running over to scoop the girls up.

'Sally Sudbury! What've you been up to? Come here this minute,' Maggie said, cuddling Sally so hard, she could barely breathe.

Pippa had never been so pleased her mother wasn't there.

'Take a seat, girls,' Brian Fitzfoster ordered. 'I'm desperately relieved to see all of you, but who's going to tell me what's been going on?'

All three girls and Twinkle looked in Maria's direction.

Oh, brilliant! Maria thought to herself. *Me again, then.*

'Dad, before I say anything, would you just read this, please?' she said, handing her dad the printed report about everything that had happened since their discovery of the Condor's egg.

Mr Fitzfoster raised an eyebrow. His clever daughter never failed to surprise him. Here he was, feeling more angry than he could remember with his girls, ready to give them the grilling of a lifetime and he'd been disarmed by two puppy dog eyes, one sentence and a couple of pieces of paper.

'I'll get us all some tea,' Maggie said, wrapping her dressing gown around her. 'Sally, be sure to tell the truth now.'

Sally nodded and smiled at her mum. She was so pleased to see her.

By the time Mr Fitzfoster reached the end of the report, his mouth was gaping slightly.

'Putting the more serious, life-threatening facts to one side for a moment, are you girls telling me there's a secret railway track running under this house?'

'Yep!' Maria said, a twinkle in her eye.

'What on earth?' Mrs Fitzfoster began as she grabbed Maria's report from her husband.

'I scarcely know where to begin with this.' Mr Fitzfoster sat and thought for a moment.

'With Albie, Dad! He's missing. I know the smugglers have got him. I just know it!' Molly said, starting to get hysterical.

'I'm presuming you're referring now to the radio message we all overheard earlier?' Mr Fitzfoster said, putting two and two together about the missing car and not so missing motorbike.

'Yes! He was supposed to go down the cliff steps, row the boat back to Barnes Bay and bring the Land Rover back to Wilton House. But he's still not back.' Sally said.

'Down the cliff steps?!' Linda Fitzfoster exclaimed. 'But you girls were specifically told this morning that the cliff steps were highly dangerous and out of bounds.'

'Yes, but Mum, don't you see, that was just the smugglers pretending to be the coastguard and sending you a message. They must have seen us watching them from the cliff-top last night and thought closing the steps would keep us away from their activities,' Maria explained.

'Right, enough is enough,' Brian Fitzfoster said. 'I'm calling the police. This whole thing is getting more and more complicated by the second. Endangered animals, smugglers, hoax messages and now a kidnapped boy.'

Mr Fitzfoster was quite red in the face as he dialled 999. The thought of having to report such a fantastic and, at the same time, serious matter to the police was daunting. At least he had Maria's report to pass on, which summed up the main events.

'The Chief Inspector is coming right away. Now, is there anything else I ought to know about what you girls have been up to? Anything at all?' Mr F continued, eyeballing each of them in turn. They shook their heads.

'We're really sorry, Dad,' Maria said softly. 'When we found that huge egg, it was all a bit of an adventure and you know how we feel about adventures . . .'

'How were we to know we'd end up in some smuggler's den in our own back garden, having to escape through a secret passage,' Sally said, appealing to her own mother who had since come back with tea and caught up.

'It does make sense of some very odd noises I've heard during the night, since coming to Wilton House,' Maggie said, looking over to Mr Fitzfoster. 'At various times, there have been some strange animal noises, but I've always just put it down to my new country life.'

Suddenly Twinkle yawned the biggest yawn, making the oddest *oooooooooow* sound as she did so. Immediately the tension in the room evaporated, and Mr Fitzfoster walked over to give his girls a hug.

'When are you two super-sleuths going to learn that life doesn't always have to be a mystery novel?' he said, squeezing them.

'We don't go out looking for trouble, Dad, honestly we don't,' Maria said as innocently as she could.

'Sure you don't!' Brian Fitzfoster said, resisting the urge to laugh. 'Right, you girls are to stay right here where your mothers can see you. I'm going to phone Malcolm and get him to meet me at the cliff steps. While we're waiting for the police to arrive, we can start by checking that Albie hasn't fallen down and broken anything.'

'Oh, Dad, that's a great idea. Here take this . . .'

Maria said, passing him her rucksack. As Mr Fitzfoster unzipped the top, two torches, a screwdriver and a hammer clattered to the floor.

'Don't ask, Dad!' Molly said and Mr Fitzfoster disappeared off to call Malcolm.

'Mrs Fitzfoster, I presume?' A tall policeman said as Linda Fitzfoster opened the front door. 'Chief Inspector Boyd,' he continued, shaking her hand.

'Yes. Hello, Chief Inspector. I'm Linda Fitzfoster. Thank you so much for coming at this late hour. Won't you come in,' Linda said, leading the way to the sitting room where everyone else was waiting patiently.

'My, my. This is quite a gathering,' Boyd said, looking over to the sofa where the girls and Twinkle were all huddled up quietly with Maggie.

'Inspector, would you be kind enough to start by reading this report my daughter has compiled, and then we'll be happy to answer your questions.'

Chief Inspector Boyd's face was a picture as Linda passed him Maria's document. He'd been trying to guess what the midnight emergency at Wilton House might be about but had drawn a complete blank, especially when he saw that the children were still awake. He had no idea what they were about to tell him.

'Can I get you some tea or coffee?' Maggie asked, kindly.

'That would be lovely, madam. Tea with two sugars, if you don't mind,' Chief Inspector Boyd answered.

'And would your men like anything?' Linda enquired, having noticed two police cars pull up outside on the drive.

'Oh, no, they'll be fine. Thank you.'

In the silence that followed, the girls were intrigued by the various facial expressions Chief Inspector Boyd pulled as he read.

'Well ladies, in all my years on the force, I can honestly say that nothing could have prepared me for this!' he said suddenly, rising out of his chair.

Linda, with a little help from the girls, went on to explain about the subsequent disappearance of poor Albie in the last hour.

'I see,' Chief Inspector Boyd said, as a windswept Brian Fitzfoster appeared in the doorway.

'Thank you for coming so quickly, Chief Inspector. Brian Fitzfoster,' he said, firmly shaking his hand. 'I presume you are now up to speed, so I'll be brief.'

'I've just checked the cliff steps and the beach but there is no sign of Albie. There are, however, *two* boats moored in the bay.'

The girls gasped.

Mr Fitzfoster continued. 'A small green rowing boat and a large blue and white motor boat.'

'It's them! They're back! The rowing boat is ours but the motor boat you describe is exactly the sort of boat we saw on Thursday night when we were spying on the bay!' Maria said.

'And I also found this?' Brian Fitzfoster said, holding up Albie's rucksack. The girls winced. 'Is this the Condor egg, Maria?' he continued, carefully removing it from Albie's bag and placing it on the coffee table.

'It is,' Maria said gravely.

'They've got poor Albie. They must have! He didn't even get a chance to make it to Barnes Bay,' Molly cried, tears rolling down her cheeks.

'She's right. It seems that Albie has been kidnapped, somewhere between leaving us at the top of the cliff and our rowing boat!' Pippa said, wide-eyed.

'What are we going to do?' Molly wailed. 'They'll probably shut him in one of the cages and forget about him.'

'Molly, get a grip! The police are here now. Albie's going to be fine,' Maria said, giving her sister a cuddle. 'That's right, isn't it, Chief Inspector?' she said.

'Mimi, the book! You've forgotten to give them the book,' Pippa said suddenly.

'Oh, yes! It's in my coat – I'll grab it,' she said and ran into the hall.

Coming back, she handed her dad the log book they'd found in the cave.

'Dad, this is all the evidence the police will need to put this smugglers away for a very long time,' she said.

Brian Fitzfoster glanced at the pages before passing it to Chief Inspector Boyd.

'Chief Inspector, if I'm not mistaken, I believe our smuggler friends have returned this evening to clear out the cave and move on. They won't want to risk waiting another night once they find their book is missing.'

'I quite agree, Mr Fitzfoster, and we shouldn't waste another moment. They could be loading up the animals as we speak. Girls, can you show us where you came out of the tunnel, so that we can try and catch these criminals in the act . . . And find your friend Albie in the process?' Chief Inspector Boyd said, looking at the four friends.

'Chief Inspector, is that really necessary? I think the girls have had quite enough criminal activity for one summer holiday,' Linda Fitzfoster said, not keen to have the girls out of her sight for another second given the current danger at Wilton House.

'Pleeeease, Mum, pleeeeease? We need to find Albie,' Molly begged. 'I won't be able to rest until I know he's safe.'

'They can come with me, dear,' Brian Fitzfoster assured her. 'Quickly, all of you go and get your coats on. Linda, you keep Twinkle in the house with you. We can't risk her barking and warning the smugglers.'

Twinkle gave a whimper but then quickly laid her exhausted head back down for a sleep.

'And Maggie, would you try phoning Malcolm again, please? I couldn't get hold of him earlier, but this isn't over and he's a good man to have on your side in times of trouble.'

Maggie nodded.

As they got into their coats, there was a gentle knock at the front door.

'Sorry to bother you, Chief Inspector. But there's movement at the end of the drive. From what we can make out, it's a large lorry but the lights are off,' said a second policeman.

'It's the getaway truck!' Maria whispered to the girls. 'Blimey it's happening! Pippa thank goodness you did forget to use channel three, or we'd never have got the police here in time to catch them.'

'What happens on channel three?' Brian Fitzfoster said, frowning at Maria. 'Don't tell me! I don't want to know. You're too clever for your own good, Miss Fitzfoster.'

'Can't think where I get it from, Dad!' Maria risked saying and moved to the front of the group. 'Follow me everyone, there's a huge hedge to one side of the tunnel exit from where we can watch without being seen. It's definitely wide enough to give us all cover. The best way to reach it is a bit long-winded, through the kitchen garden and out the back, but this way we avoid the drive completely. If there's someone watching the area from that truck, we can't risk being spotted.'

Chief Inspector Boyd listened in astonishment at the way this young lady seemed to be taking charge of his investigation. He felt as if he was in one of the Famous Five novels he used to read as a child. Five children and a dog solving crimes before the police even had a sniff that something was going on.

'Slow down, Maria. I promised your mum I'd keep

you close!' Brian Fitzfoster whispered as he crept past Maggie's runner beans.

But Maria was off, followed closely by Boyd and three uniformed policemen.

'Over here,' she whispered, crouching behind the hedge.

'Excellent location, Miss Fitzfoster,' Chief Inspector Boyd whispered to a glowing Maria. Then he turned to his men. 'Smith – you go with Forbes and position yourselves in those trees on the other side of the drive. We need to spread out a bit in case the smugglers decide to make a run for it. Parker, you stay here with me. And for goodness sake mute the volume on your radios. Last thing we need is dispatch calling when we're mid stake-out!'

'Here – use our walkie-talkie watches,' Maria said. 'You'll be able to stay in contact with each other without risk of outsiders calling in unexpectedly.'

The girls handed Smith and Forbes two of their watches and watched as they disappeared back towards the house to their new hiding positions.

'Stake-out!' Sally whispered to Pippa, her heart pounding. 'It's not just in the movies. They really do say that!'

'Shhhhh!' Boyd snapped.

They crouched silently, looking back and forth from the tunnel exit to the vague outline of a large truck, parked in the dark. So far they hadn't seen anyone else. They'd just have to wait.

'What time do you make it, Parker?'

'1.34 am,' Maria piped up. She couldn't help herself. If someone asked a question, she always had an overwhelming urge to answer it.

Boyd looked at Maria in surprise and then at Parker. What he really wanted to say was 'Is your name, Parker?' but he thought better of it.

'1.34 am, sir,' Parker agreed.

'Girls, I think I'd better take you back to the house. It's getting far too late and chilly out here.' Brian Fitzfoster said protectively.

'Nooooo! Dad, please. You promis . . .'

'Shhhhhh!' Chief Inspector Boyd hissed suddenly, and held up his hand. Maria could only assume this was a police signal to his colleagues to show that something was happening.

'Stand by, boys . . . Boyd whispered into his watch.

'Roger that . . .' Smith's voice whispered back.

Thud, thud, thud, came three loud bangs from the direction of the hatch.

'I don't know why they're banging — the hatch isn't locked. It only bolted from the inside, and once we were out we had to leave it open...' Pippa whispered.

Chief Inspector Boyd looked at her, eager for any extra information.

'Actually, that's not strictly true. I rolled one of those big, pine logs from the shed onto the hatch before we left. I was just thinking about stopping any smugglers from getting out at the time,' Sally said, feeling as if she'd let the side down.

'Oh, don't worry . . . We weren't to know we'd be back here actually hoping to see a smuggler!' Molly said.

'I'd have done the same thing if I'd have thought of it, Sally!' Pippa said, giving her a hug.

Thud, thud, thud!

'Shhhhh!' Boyd hissed again and then whispered into his watch. 'They're getting close, I heard the log shift that time.'

Thud, thud . . . creak . . . crash!

Everyone watched in silence as the hatch flew open and crashed onto the ground.

A head covered entirely by a massive furry hood popped out of the hatch and scanned the area.

'Clear!' he whispered, jumping out onto the grass.

'It's Skinny Smuggler,' Maria breathed. 'He's the one who disappeared on the beach. There's at least one more in there that we know of.'

Boyd nodded. He was poised like a leopard ready to pounce on its prey.

'Move on my signal, boys,' he instructed calmly into the watch. 'We wait until they are all out in the open before we go . . .'

'Push her out!' Skinny Smuggler whispered, loudly enough for them all to hear. They watched him drag a medium sized wooden crate out of the tunnel and onto the grass.

Molly held her breath. She was desperate to know which one of those poor animals was inside.

'Next!' Skinny Smuggler called out. Suddenly another crate appeared in the tunnel opening and was dragged out into the moonlight.

'Let's get them all out before we get her to bring the truck down,'

Her? Maria thought. 'Oh, my gosh, it's a woman driving that truck!' she whispered in surprise.

We're not entirely sure why everyone had assumed the smugglers would be men, Story-seeker, but there you go.

They continued to watch in silence as one by one, Skinny Smuggler dragged the crates onto the grass.

'Is this the last one?' Skinny Smuggler asked, wiping his nose on his sleeve.

There was a muffled response from the other side of the hatch before the big smuggler climbed out into the open.

'One more,' he grunted.

Both men bent forwards and heaved the final crate out of the hatch together.

'I bet that's the tiger!' Maria whispered as quietly as she could.

Inspector Boyd was revving up to go. 'Wait for the truck and then move on my signal,' he spoke into the watch.

'Roger that,' came an even quieter response from Smith.

Suddenly the big smuggler's phone lit up as he put it to his hooded ear. 'Sue, get down here now!' No sooner had he hung up than the truck started to move towards them in the darkness.

'Sue?' Molly breathed, a horrendous thought crossing her mind. 'You don't think . . .'

'No,' Maria answered. 'No, it can't be . . . it couldn't be . . . Could it?'

The girls fell silent as the truck pulled to a stop and the door opened metres from where they were hiding. As the driver emerged, the twin's worst fears were confirmed. But they didn't have time to share their discovery.

'Go, go, go!' Boyd whispered into the watch, dropping his hand as though it was a flag starting a race.

Boyd and Parker raced out, flanking the two smugglers and the driver on one side, while Smith and Forbes matched their manouevre from the opposite side.

'Stop! Police!' Boyd shouted fiercely. The smugglers tried to move but they couldn't. They were outnumbered and completely surrounded, and they knew it.

'Put your hands on the side of the truck . . . do it . . . now!' Parker boomed as the three criminals moved toward the truck, their hands in the air in surrender.

Very quickly, Smith and Forbes moved in with their handcuffs, while Chief Inspector Boyd read them their rights.

'I am arresting you on suspicion of smuggling endangered species into the country, and kidnap. You have the right to remain silent when questioned but anything you say or do may be used against you in a court of law . . . '

'Susie, how could you!' Maria shouted, slipping her dad's hand and running towards the truck. 'We trusted you. Mum and Dad trusted you.'

'Maria!' Brian Fitzfoster called out, as he tried to grab Maria by the shoulder. He hadn't noticed the identity of the driver, but as he got closer, it was suddenly clear to Mr Fitzfoster why Maria was so angry and his face fell in shock.

'Do you recognise any of these people here this evening, sir?' Boyd asked, pulling down the men's hoods to reveal their faces. When Boyd had seen Maria's reaction to the female driver, he immediately assumed it was an inside job. It usually was.

'I'm sorry to say I do, Inspector,' Brian Fitzfoster

answered solemnly, feeling as though he'd been punched in the stomach. 'Their names are Malcolm and Tom Kent and they are the father and son caretakers at Wilton House. And this woman, their getaway driver is called Susie, our retired ex-housekeeper.' He shook his head in despair.

'Where's Albie?' Molly screamed suddenly at Malcolm. 'What have you done with him?'

A terrified-looking Tom nodded over to the crates still standing on the grass.

'Help me someone, he's in one of the crates! Help me!' Maria cried, running over to them. She saw frightened eyes staring up at her through the slats. But then she heard a light snoring coming from inside another crate. 'Here!' she cried. 'Albie, can you hear me! Oh, Albie, please wake up. We're coming!'

'Let me,' Parker said, levering off the lid.

By this time, all four girls were peering through the crate at a seemingly peaceful, sleeping, Albie.

'What did you do to him?' Maria shouted angrily at Malcolm.

'It's just a sleeping pill. He's fine. Ran smack into him on that beach and he just wouldn't keep quiet so we had to shut him up for a bit. No harm done, you'll see.'

'No harm done? We'll see what the judge has to say about that!' Maria spat.

'Albie!' Maria and Molly squealed as Parker hauled him out and gently laid him on the grass. 'Albie wake up!'

'Best call an ambulance, sir, just to be on the safe side,' Parker suggested to Chief Inspector Boyd.

'Of course,' Boyd answered, signalling to Forbes and Smith to watch the prisoners.

'Wha . . . what time is it?' Albie stammered, slowly trying to open his eyes. 'I've got . . . got to get to work.'

'Oh, Albie, Albie, we're so sorry. You've been so brave,' Molly said.

'You're safe now,' Pippa said, patting his hair. 'The paramedics are on their way to do a check up. The smugglers gave you a sleeping tablet to keep you quiet but it's nothing serious.'

Albie looked up at all the alarmed faces staring down at him and grinned his biggest, cheekiest grin. 'Like I said before, girls. You sure do know how to party!'

'Chief Inspector, thank you so much for your efforts here tonight. Can we leave you to deal with this situation? I think it best I get these girls and Albie back to the house for a cup of hot chocolate, before we all pass out with adrenalin and tiredness. You and your men have been first rate this evening.'

'Thank you, sir. That means a lot coming from you. If you don't mind though sir, I'd like to return in the morning to take statements from you and your little detectives. If any of them fancies a job on the police force one day, I'd be delighted to provide a reference! I'd also like to take a look at that cave and secret railway if I may?' Boyd said with a boyish grin.

'You and me both!' Brian Fitzfoster exclaimed, desperate to see the secrets that lay under his home by the sea. 'We'll see you in the morning then, Chief Inspector.'

And with that, the Fitzfosters and their extended family made their way back to the open arms of Linda and Maggie, and a cauldron of steaming cocoa.

18

What Exactly Happened Last Night?

'Albie!' Molly jumped up from the breakfast table. 'How did you sleep?'

'Ha! You look like you like you've had a fight – or a fright!' Sally giggled, seeing Albie's hair all matted and standing on end.

'Errr, it might well be a case of all of the above I think. It was a night full of fight *and* fright!' Albie smiled.

'Good morning, Albie, dear. Please have a seat. Would you like some orange juice?' Mrs Fitzfoster asked.

'That would be lovely, thank you. I'm gasping,' Albie said, sitting between Molly and Pippa. 'And thanks so much for putting me up last night – and for phoning my boss to explain why I won't be in today. I definitely couldn't have driven back to London last night. My head feels as if it's been in a boxing ring by itself!'

'That will be the sleeping draft the smugglers gave you,' Mrs Fitzfoster said, shaking her head. She still couldn't quite believe what had been happening right under her nose.

'Where's Maria?' Albie asked, suddenly noticing one of the gang was missing.

'Oh, you know, Maria. She was up at the crack of dawn putting together an exclusive for the local paper. Then once she'd emailed that over, copying in Luscious Tangerella of course, she scooted off to the beach with Dad and Chief Inspector Boyd to give them the grand, and no doubt detailed, tour! I can just see her now, documenting our every move - from where we originally spotted the Condor egg, to discovering the hidden doughnut entrance to the cave itself, and finally Wilton's best kept secret railway!' Molly said, relieved she hadn't had to go with them. She'd had enough exploring for one summer holiday.

'I bet she hasn't mentioned the lack of electrics on that railway! Hope your dad and the Chief Inspector are ready to lose the use of their arms for twenty-four hours. I can barely hold my knife and fork without them shaking!' Sally said with a giggle.

'Girls, Albie, all joking aside, I can hardly bear to hear your stories from last night. What if one of you had been seriously hurt?' Mrs Fitzfoster asked. 'You really have got to take your safety more seriously. These situations you manage to get yourselves into would be dangerous for any grown up, let alone for children your age.'

'I know, Mum,' Molly agreed, walking over to her mother's chair to give her a big hug. 'And you're right. I think we all had a bit of a scare this time around. Particularly when Albie went missing. We just didn't expect the mystery to be so huge and so dangerous, when we started out.'

'You've got to promise me, Molly, that next time you're faced with a mystery, you involve either your father and me or another adult immediately, rather than doing ninety-nine percent of the investigating by yourselves before asking for help,' Linda continued, giving her daughter her sternest look.

'I promise, Mum,' Molly said, truthfully. But she couldn't speak for her super-sleuth sister.

'I know, let's take Twinkle for a run around in the top field behind the garages. We'll be able to spot when Maria and Dad come out of the tunnel,' Molly said as they lay sunbathing outside Hotel L'Etoile having brought Albie down to show him their summer holiday home.

'Great idea. I'll just grab my trainers,' Sally said, running inside.

'Your family is so cool, Molly,' Albie said.

'Ah, thanks, Albietross. It's our pleasure. Who knows what would have happened to us if you hadn't been there. It might have been one of us in that crate,' Molly said, wincing at the thought.

'What did happen to you after we left you at the cliff steps?' Pippa asked.

'Well it's all a bit of a blur, really, but I know where I went wrong. I was in such a hurry to reach the boat that I totally forgot to check the beach for any other boats in the bay. I remember getting down to the beach and just as I was about to get my waders out of my bag to walk out to the boat, I ran smack, bang into your mate Tom. We were both running and it was so dark, we nearly knocked each other out!' Albie said, squinting in the sunlight.

'You must have been terrified! Then what happened!' Molly asked.

'Next thing I knew, there were two of them dragging me kicking and screaming through the sand, and up and over the rock to the doughnut hole. Then I remember one of them ramming some sort of tablet in my mouth and minutes later I was out for the count. After that, you three were standing over me in the moonlight.'

'Ah, kind of romantic when you put it like that!' Pippa said.

'Hardly, Pips!' Molly cried. 'Thank goodness it was only a sleeping tablet. They might have tried to poison you, or anything to keep you quiet!'

Albie smiled. What an adventure! His mates were never going to believe it!

'OK, let's go!' Sally shouted, slamming the door behind her. 'Last one to the hatch is going to have a bad hair day for the wedding tomorrow!'

'The wedding!' Pippa and Molly cried in genuine

horror. They'd forgotten all about it!

Pippa looked at her watch. 'Oh, my goodness, this time tomorrow, I'll be minutes away from singing. Right now I can't even remember the song's title, let alone the words.'

'Don't worry, it'll all come back to you. Come on, let's go and get Maria. Then we'll all come back to Hotel L'Etoile and dedicate the rest of the afternoon to trying on our new outfits, complete with hair and make-up. But, most importantly, we'll help you rehearse until you're re-hoarse! Ha, get it . . . hoarse?' Molly said, laughing. But Pippa was too panicky to hear the joke. The song lyrics had begun to take shape in her head and she found herself humming the tune.

'Come on, my little humming-bird. To the hatch!' Sally said and they ran off to join the others.

Molly, Pippa, Sally, Albie and Twinkle were just in time to see Maria pop her head out of the hatch and jokingly call out *clear!* just like Tom had done only hours before.

'Molly!' she cried as she spied her sister and the others. 'Moll, you guys should have come with us. It was even more amazing this time. The whole cave is crawling with forensic and RSPCA investigators. In fact, Chief Inspector Boyd needs all of our prints – isn't that right, Chief Inspector?' she said to a rather sweaty man exiting the hatch.

'Indeed, Miss Fitzfoster,' he panted, approaching them. Seeing Sally look worried, he explained. 'It's just to eliminate your prints from others we've found at the scene. Malcolm Kent hasn't said a word since Parker took him to the station, but Tom Kent's proving a little easier to crack. It would seem that there are a number of other locals involved in this smuggling ring, so we'll need forensics to help build our case against them.'

'Chief Inspector, what's happened to all the animals?' Molly asked. She'd been desperate to find that out since leaving last night.

'The RSPCA are working with our animal control branch to rehome them to various animal shelters where they will live out the rest of their lives peacefully and happily. You stumbled on quite an operation here at Wilton Bay. Thanks to that log book you cleverly found and retained, Maria, it seems that the Kents have been significant players in the illegal trade of exotic birds and animals to the UK for generations.'

'Who would have believed it? I certainly can't,'

Sally said. From the little she'd got to know of Tom and his dad since arriving at Wilton House at the beginning of the summer she just couldn't believe they were involved in something so hideous.

'I'm afraid that comes with the territory. Life is full of surprises, and not all of them good ones. You'd do well to remember that, all of you, when you next decide to embark on an *adventure* alone,' Boyd concluded.

'Very well said, Chief Inspector,' Mr Fitzfoster agreed. 'Girls, I can't begin to express to you how important it is that you don't make a habit of putting yourselves and your friends in danger. Is that clear?'

'Yes, Dad,' the twins mumbled.

'Yes, Mr Fitzfoster,' Albie, Pippa and Sally nodded.

'Very good. And now for the fun part,' Mr Fitzfoster went on.

'Daddy?' Molly asked.

'What on earth are we going to do with this new-found adventure playground below us? I say we get some engineers in to make the whole thing safe by Christmas and then throw a party. What do you say?' Brian Fitzfoster said, a glint in his eye.

'Woooohooo!' Molly squealed.

'Brilliant!' Maria said, already thinking how she

could invite Luscious and the Gazette down to have exclusive access to the cave and the railway.

'We could even use the party to raise money for the animal charities who are going to take care of the animals from the cave!' Sally said, thoughtfully.

'Sally Sudbury, that is an excellent idea!' said Brian Fitzfoster.' That's your next school holiday project taken care of then, girls. That should be enough to keep you out of mischief for a while,'

I flipping hope not! Maria thought to herself. There was always time for mischief!

19

Here Comes The Bride . . .

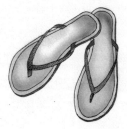

'Pippa . . . stop fidgeting,' Molly whispered as she stood at her terrified friend's side. 'Not only do you look like an angel, when have you ever not sung like one?'

'What if I let everyone down? I've never felt pressure like this. It's their wedding day, it has to be perfect,' Pippa said, trembling.

'And it will be. You can do this,' Molly said, looking up the aisle. Even Mr Fuller didn't look as nervous as Pippa. In fact he looked rather calm and handsome as he waited for his bride to join him.

Molly ran over to where Maria and Sally were sitting.

'Whasssup?' Maria asked.

'It's Pippa. The nerves are totally getting the better of her. I've never seen her like this before. I'm worried, Mimi. What if she starts to sing and no sound comes out? I've read about things like this. People choke all the time in auditions,' Molly said, starting to sound as out of control as Pippa.

'Molly you sit down. I've got this,' Sally said, jumping up from her seat and before either twin could say a word she was at Pippa's side whispering in her ear.

'What do you think she's saying?' Molly said.

'I've no idea, but it looks like it's working!' Maria said smiling, as she watched Pippa's whole face change from tormented to happy in seconds!

Sally gave the girls a wink. Nerves and conquering them had been her forte since having to host the homeless charity auction at the end of last term. If someone had told her she'd be the *hostess with the mostess* at such a prestigious event when she'd started out at L'Etoile as Lucifette's timid sidekick, she'd have laughed in their face.

Dum, dum, dee, dum . . . dum, dum, dee, dum . . . came the oh-so familiar bridal march of *Here Comes the Bride*.

The congregation gasped with delight as they caught their first glimpse of the blushing bride.

'She looks divine,' Molly whispered.

Molly, despite her young years, Story-seeker had been planning her own wedding for as long as she could remember and she had to say that so far, Miss Hart's plans were out-shining her own! Something she'd have to put right at a later date!

'And have you ever seen a more proud father?' Maria said, looking first at Mr Hart and then glancing at her own dad.

Mr Hart had returned from his trip to Iceland the day before to join his daughter and new son-in-law for the wedding. He'd been so emotional that morning, without Twinkle there for moral support, that he was terrified he'd turn into a blubbering wreck as he walked his little girl down the aisle but so far, so good!

As the vicar finished the first part of the service, he invited the happy couple and congregation to take their seats to listen to a very special, personal performance from *the angelic* Pippa Burrows.

Sally gave Pippa a wink and Pippa, her face alight with pride and happiness, stepped up to the podium where the pianist was ready to accompany her.

'What the heck did Sally say to her?' Maria whispered to Molly.

'I dunno . . . but let's hope we can bottle it and sell

it!' Molly said and fell silent as the melody began to fill the church. Pippa's voice floated up to the ceiling, hanging in the air like the flower garlands looped through the rafters. It was as though the guests were holding their breath so as not to interrupt the song.

Just you and I
Our lives entwined
Begin our story together
Just you and I forever
Through love
True love

And as she concluded the final note, the church, appropriately or not given the solemn venue, erupted into rapturous applause.

Pippa smiled as Miss Hart blew her a kiss and Mr Fuller nodded in delight. She knew she'd done well. She felt good!

'Hurrah! Hurrah!' the guests cheered as the new Mr and Mrs Fuller exited the church to billows of petal confetti.

Everyone was smiling and desperate to congratulate

them. The happiness was infectious.

'Pippa!' Molly and Maria cried, running up to Pippa and Sally who suddenly appeared from the church.

'Pippa I don't know what to say,' Molly said. 'Your performance was amazing!'

'Ah, thanks. But I couldn't have done it without dear Sally! You saw me Molly. I was a wreck. If she hadn't have come over when she did I really think I would have fainted with fear!'

'Sally – come on, spill the beans – what on earth did you say to Pippa to make her flip like that,' Maria asked.

'I just told Pippa to do what I did before I opened my mouth on that podium at the charity auction last term…' Sally said.

'Which was what?' Molly said.

'Imagining the look on Madame Ruby's face if Twinkle were to suddenly jump up and run off with her wig!' Sally said at which point all four girls exploded into a much needed fit of giggles.

'Oh, Sally, you do make me laugh. You really do have funny bones,' Molly said, pulling herself together.

'Well, thank goodness one of us does, or we'd all be a bunch of serious wrecks! What a team!' Pippa said, high-fiving her bestest friends in the world.

'My, my L'Etoilettes, I love nothing better than a bit of camaraderie, but this is neither the time, nor the place for such sports venue antics.' The girls swung around to see Madame Ruby tottering in all her finery, an immaculately groomed wig clinging to her immaculately painted face. Only Maria managed to hold it together enough to address their headmistress.

'Madame Ruby. What a pleasure it is to see you ahead of the new term. You must be feeling extraordinarily proud today of Miss Hart,' Maria said with a completely straight face.

'Oh, yes,' Molly joined in. 'Doesn't she look like a princess. I just love what she's done with her hair, don't you?' She couldn't help herself but bring the conversation back around to hair dos. Pippa tried to smother a giggle.

'And you, Miss Burrows,' Madame Ruby said, turning to Pippa. 'I must say exquisite song choice and execution on your part. I look forward to hearing more excellent writing from you this year.'

'Of course, Madame. I shall do my best,' Pippa said, practically curtseying.

'And you, Fitzfoster L'Etoilettes? Am I to have the honour of escorting your parents on their personal *Legend of the Lost Rose* tour when you return for school tomorrow afternoon? The tours have been a phenomenal success this summer, so I'm looking forward to showing them the part you played in all this,' Madame Ruby continued.

Great, Maria thought. That's all her mum and dad needed tomorrow . . . Another reminder of exactly how much mischief they got up to when they were out of sight. Especially when the last major mischief only concluded last night!

'Oh, Madame Ruby, I'm sure my parents would be delighted, but I'm not sure tomorrow is going to be the best time for them. They've made a discovery of their own at the house in the country this week, and I have a feeling they'll be tied up there for a little while yet,' Maria said, trying her best to stop Madame Ruby from having a conversation with her parents at all. But sadly it backfired!

'Discovery of their own, you say? How interesting. And would I be correct in assuming that the four of you were instrumental in that discovery too?' she asked, raising an eyebrow.

The girls couldn't bring themselves to answer for fear of digging themselves a further hole.

'Just as I thought, L'Etoilettes. Let's all hope for a successful and discovery-free second year at L'Etoile.

Until tomorrow then,' and with that she swooshed on her heels in the direction of Mr and Mrs Fitzfoster.

'Oh, no, we're for it now. As much as dad finds old Ruby tiresome, I don't fancy our chances when they get together and realise not only are we scheming little witches at school, we're like it at home as well!' Maria groaned.

'Look, let's not worry about that now. We've got a few hours left of these summer holidays and I for one want to enjoy them! Who's in?'

'Me!' Pippa and Sally replied.

'Right then, let's start by going to congratulate the bride and groom and then eating as many ice-creams as the guy manning the stand will give us!' Molly said, smoothing back her hair as she always did when she was ready for action. 'Flakes too, obvs!'

'What a summer this has been,' Sally said. 'Thank you so much for everything, girls. Best friends forever?'

'BFFs!' the others exclaimed.